D1226249

THE CONTEMPORARY
ART OF THE NOVELLA

THE CONTEMPORARY ART OF THE NOVELLA

CLOSE TO JEDENEW

CLOSE TO JEDENEW

KEVIN VENNEMANN

TRANSLATED BY ROSS BENJAMIN

MELVILLEHOUSE
BROOKLYN, NEW YORK

FIRST PUBLISHED AS *NAHE JEDENEW* (© SUHRKAMP VERLAG
FRANKFURT AM MAIN).

COPYRIGHT © KEVIN VENNEMANN 2008

TRANSLATION © ROSS BENJAMIN 2008

THE PUBLICATION OF THIS WORK WAS SUPPORTED BY A GRANT
FROM THE GOETHE-INSTITUT.

BOOK DESIGN: BLAIR AND HAYES, BASED ON A SERIES DESIGN BY
DAVID KONOPKA

MELVILLE HOUSE PUBLISHING
145 PLYMOUTH STREET
BROOKLYN, NY 11201

WWW.MHPBOOKS.COM

ISBN: 978-1-933633-39-8

FIRST MELVILLE HOUSE PRINTING: JULY 2008

A CATALOG RECORD FOR THIS BOOK IS AVAILABLE FROM THE
LIBRARY OF CONGRESS.

CLOSE TO JEDENEW

We do not breathe. The place is close to Jedenew, we hear the Jedenew farmers singing, bawling, playing clarinet, accordion, we hear their songs for hours already, old partisan songs, they play and sing and bawl in a strangely melodious fashion. For hours the Jedenew farmers sit in the woods behind the house and drink and laugh and sing and play, and only after hours go by do we finally hear them coming out of the woods, singing at the top of their voices and marching over the ridge into the garden. At night the windows in the kitchen rattle, then every single window in the house rattles. In the evening we sit behind the house in the midsummer evening sun on the narrow wooden dock that leads out into the pond behind the house, we sit and lie and swim in the sun and sit together reading and drink the first and last summer punch of the year, swim and splash one another with water, at night we crouch in our bathing suits, crammed into the pantry. In the evening we sit, nine in number, at night we are six, counting Zygmunt and Julia, though Marek says that Zygmunt and Julia are still much too little to count. To take away Zygmunt's fear, Marek says: If they get us, they're going to take only us four. In the evening we listen to Father, who reads fairy tales, old legends, poems, at night we hear the Jedenew farmers singing, playing, marching in disorder. In the evening we count the mosquito bites on our legs and braid each other's hair, at night we crouch, crammed into the pantry. In the evening we lie in the grass behind the house stretched out in the sun, at night we shift awkwardly as quietly as possible onto our knees, one after another since there's only enough space in the pantry for one person at a time to kneel. In the evening we take Zygmunt by his arms and legs and, laughing, throw him with a great swing into the pond, at night we kneel and see, through the crack between the floor and the pantry door, the blue-white moonlight scattered on the kitchen floor, we hear the Jedenew farmers singing and playing clarinet, accordion, as if they were standing directly beside us, and see their shadows, nineteen altogether, cut up in the shattered glass all over the floor, slowly passing by the window, we do not breathe, we think: We are six, counting Zygmunt and little Julia, though we can't really count either of them, as Marek says, they're certainly not going to take Zygmunt and Julia, says Marek, to take away Zygmunt and Julia's fear, we think: They are nineteen, Sapetow is among them, Kaczmarek, Varta, Sieminski, Geniek, Dzielski and Sobuta are among them, even the Kradejew veterinarian, we think: Naturally Krystowczyk is among them, and think: First of all Krystowczyk has only one eye. Secondly he is well over sixty and slow in his movements, we think: Nothing remains for him but to catch us here in the pantry, somewhere else, out of the pantry, outside, he can't get us. We hear, they pass beyond the house, we hear, farther down the street they sing and play an age-old German hiking song, their singing is a compass for us, and their German sounds strange, the way they'd speak after learning it only recently, today, yesterday, after picking it up somewhere by chance, entirely in passing, when in fact they speak German already for centuries. We hear Krystowczyk singing, speaking, bawling loudest, much louder than the others, and giving orders in German, only last week, in mid-June, Father and Marek drive out to Krystowczyk's farm to slaughter twenty-five of Krystowczyk's pigs dying of pig plague, and during the slaughter Krystowczyk sings softly in Russian, no doubt to mock us, Marek and me, says Father in the evening. And then at night, already tonight, Krystowczyk sings, speaks, bawls, gives orders as well as he can in German, we hear him and the others arriving in front of Wasznar and Antonina's farm with loud jubilant cries, and hear Krystowczyk ordering the others in German to set the fire, we do not breathe. We crouch, crammed into the pantry, resting our elbows on our knees, and taking turns we see, through the crack under the door, the moon, blue-white, torn to pieces in the window slivers. We hear them falling silent, and then hear all nineteen howling and bawling and shooting again and again into the air with glee, and in the slivers and shards on the floor and in the small amount of glass remaining in the window-frame Wasznar and Antonina's farm goes up in blue-white flames, we do not breathe. Marek takes Zygmunt on his arm. Antonina takes little, sleeping Julia on her arm, we come out of the pantry into the kitchen. Marek almost has to prevent Antonina by force from beginning to sweep up the shards and slivers with Julia on her arm, he throws the broom, the metal dustpan, to the floor and pulls Antonina along behind him. It is very hot, the sky behind the poplars in the garden and behind the pines in the woods and behind the oaks and behind the spruces and behind the beeches in the woods is bright as day from the fire, and before our eyes and over the grass in the garden there is fog. We do not breathe, we spend not much more than a second or two in the blue-white steam of the kitchen, but we count to one hundred, we count to one thousand, we stand at the kitchen table, we lean on Katarzyna's counter, we rest our forearms on the backs of the chairs, we tap with our fingernails carefully against the still half-full glass bowl of summer punch sitting on the kitchen table, at night the punch sloshes back and forth in the bowl, in the evening, on the last evening, we drink from the punch, each of us a glassful, in the evening, on the last evening, on the wooden dock behind the house Antonina suddenly says softly: They're coming, and when we jump up, run away, our punch glasses fall into the water or shatter on the wooden dock or spill out over Father's books, some of the books fall into the water as we run away, we do not breathe. At night we touch the bowl carefully with our fingernails in the blue-white steam of the kitchen, making a sound that drowns in Wasznar's loudly crackling farm. We stand leaning against the oven, Marek and Anna stand together leaning against the kitchen door, and we count to one hundred, and we count to one thousand, and we count until Marek cries Now, and starts to run, and so we run behind him, stumble through the garden behind the house and over the ridge behind the house toward the woods, toward the field, and Antonina with little Julia on her arm twists her ankle and falls and remains lying in tears on the path that we cut in the field in May, and lays her head in her arms, as we could see if we'd turn around, but we do not turn around, we keep running, we run into the field and think: She falls, she lays her head in her arms, as we could see if we'd turn around, but we do not turn around, we keep running, we run into the field, we think: She falls, she lays her head in her arms, as we could see if we'd turn around, but we do not turn around, we keep running, we run into the field, we think: We are running without turning around even one more time to Antonina. Marek has a long kitchen knife, a bread knife. Here and there he hacks what stands in the way as he runs, and on all fours we reach our clearing, we sing, it is May. We sing, and as we sing we unfold the tablecloth on the ground in the field, Marek sticks his kitchen knife, his bread knife into his pocket, and lays the scythe in such a way that Zygmunt can't step on it. Marek lies down and stretches out, he is tall, the mowed circle is just wide enough for long Marek, Antonina lays her head on his chest, Anna lays her head on Antonina's belly and hears Julia kicking. Antonina passes out the food while we sing softly. Marek says: Lie down, I want to tell you about shooting buzzards, and over there on the path that we cut in the field in May, little Julia starts to scream as the Jedenew farmers and the Kradejew veterinarian, all nineteen of them, singing, bawling, playing, tug at her. Anna, between us, cries out and jumps up, and Marek presses his hand over her mouth and pushes her under him with all his strength to the ground, then lets her go, stumbles and recovers his balance and wants to run back alone through the grain to Antonina and Julia, then the singing, bawling, playing fall silent directly before us on the path that we cut in the field only a few weeks ago in May. Julia screams, she is still a baby and screams as babies just scream without knowing why. She is still screaming in the distance when Marek crouches again beside us, shakes his head, digs his fingers into his hair, Anna's hand lies on his shoulder, we do not breathe, we see the small, bright moons of the Jedenew farmers' torches floating along the dirt road back to the house, and duck down just in time as they shine a lantern over the field. A wind blows over the field, the grain dances, and looked at long enough with teary eyes, it stands rigid as bars. We hear a dragging in the distance and Antonina suddenly screeching so that it hurts, we hear something falling into the pond in the garden behind the house or hear the Jedenew farmers throwing something into the pond in the garden behind the house, we hear Antonina jumping into the water and coming back out, jumping back in and climbing out again screeching, we hear the Jedenew farmers laughing, bawling, and as we cower in our clearing we hear Krystowczyk's voice booming the loudest of all the voices among nineteen voices, we hear Krystowczyk's voice laughing before all eighteen others, Krystowczyk speaks and shouts and laughs at the same time, and Marek whispers: Now Antonina is standing by the pond and turning around toward us and looking across the blue-white fields, and she sees little Julia before her swimming facedown in the pond, and sees the same grain moving in the wind as we do, sees before her little Julia slowly drifting to the other shore. And sees the fog before her eyes and over the fields, even before the eyes of the Jedenew farmers, steaming blue-white, exactly as we too see it, he says: The same field, the same grain, the same moon, the same night, the same fog, Marek says: The fog saves us tonight, he says: She is looking around for us and waiting for us, Marek holds us back by the wrists, he says: But we can't come, and we shut our eyes and think: She is looking around for us and waiting for us, we think: We can't come. We keep our eyes shut, Marek's rings dig into our wrists, as Antonina stops screeching in the distance. Marek's rings in our wrists, we hear Antonina jumping, hear how the water resists while we count, we count for only a second, count to ten thousand and beyond, hear how the water fights with Antonina, then hear nothing more, and Marek murmurs: An idea. At night he pulls us along behind him by the wrists to Father's car parked unattended on the dirt road. At night Anna holds Zygmunt on her arm and with her free hand holds his little boy's mouth shut, Marek turns around to her and whispers over the crackling of the fire: Not too tight, and then, because she doesn't understand him, shouts over the crackling of the fire: Not too tight, and even over the crackling of the fire we hear the Jedenew farmers standing behind the house by the pond amid punch glasses, books, towels, and singing, bawling, playing clarinet, accordion, we hear them singing and playing clarinet, accordion, we hear their songs for hours already, old partisan and German hiking songs, they sing and bawl in a strangely melodious fashion. In the evening Marek takes little Julia from Wasznar and rocks her until she falls asleep in his arms, he says: Their voices, the voices of former partisans, are now nothing more than the voices of conforming, secret patriots, Marek says hoarsely: Today they are glad just to be left in peace if they only have to do a little dirty work for it. He points to the place on the ridge where the dirt road leads onto it and runs into the street to Jedenew as a dozen trucks from Jedenew turn onto the dirt road and head toward our house and Wasznar's burning farm. In our kitchen the remaining windows shatter. Then every single window in the house shatters.

We hear one of the Jedenew farmers climbing down into the pond and, laughing, bawling, coming back out, and so we follow Marek the last few meters through the field onto the dirt road toward Father's car parked unattended on the dirt road, we follow Marek out of the field onto the open dirt road and across the dirt road, a good stretch along the dirt road, and are still following him even as he pummels dripping wet, laughing, waiting Krystowczyk. We do not breathe, we do not speak, it is hot. We lie in the circle of the clearing, we do not look at each other, we ask without speaking: What now. We lie in the circle of the clearing, the two of us, the two of us have ample space in the clearing, we are younger and smaller than Marek, we help Marek mow the circle in the field in May, the two of us take the scythe and want to lay the scythe in such a way that Zygmunt can't step on it,

Marek helps us, and then the three of us take the scythe, finally Marek alone takes the scythe and lays the scythe in such a way that Zygmunt can't step on it. Anna leans forward without moving, she is not even one meter away, but the fog is so thick that she disappears in the fog, Anna asks without speaking: What do we do now. We do not speak, but what we do: We sit and stand up only for a few moments to stretch, and crouch back to back and lie down on our backs and lie down on our bellies and lie down on our sides and lie down on our backs and draw our knees to our chests as we lie, and stand up carefully and look carefully across the grain and see Wasznar and Antonina's farm burning not even all too far away, and lie across each other like an X on our backs and lie like a T taking turns laying our heads on each other's bellies, and crawl to the edge of the clearing so as to see something and crawl carefully a few meters into the grain so as to see something and test which of us two dares go farther into the grain, and play with Marek's long kitchen knife, his bread knife, and teach ourselves how to stab with it, and teach ourselves how to cut away with it the grain that stands in the way as we run by, and teach ourselves how to cut away with it the grain that stands in the way as we run by fleeing, and teach ourselves how to hold each other as long and quietly as possible in a headlock, and lie down and breathe as quietly as possible and move forward as quietly as possible in the circle of the clearing, and jump up as quietly as possible and venture into the grain almost as far as the place on the dirt road where Marek lies, and try to move along in the grain as quietly as possible without losing our orientation, and

lie down and lie beside each other and take turns
sleeping while the one on watch keeps watch, and jump
up again and again during our watch as quietly as possible
at even the slightest sound, and finally both fall asleep
for only a moment and then lie awake for the greater
part of the night, holding each other's hands. Anna asks:
What do we do now, otherwise we do not speak. Anna
takes Marek's kitchen knife, his bread knife, and wipes
the knife soundlessly on a cluster of grain as she runs by.
On the ridge we pass very near our house, we hear the
Jedenew farmers talking. Anna wipes the knife
soundlessly on cornstalk leaves as she runs by, we hear
the Jedenew farmers speaking with the soldiers and
wonder if Zygmunt is perhaps already among them, and
wonder, if not, where Zygmunt may be now. We creep
carefully over the ridge where the growth is sparse and
creep carefully somewhat nearer still so as to hear what
the Jedenew farmers are discussing with the soldiers, we
crawl carefully somewhat nearer still so as to understand
something, so as to find out perhaps something about
Zygmunt, over Wasznar's loudly crackling farm we
understand nothing. We hear them talking, the Jedenew
farmers talk Polish to one another, they talk in halting
German with the soldiers, Wasznar's farm crackles, we
understand nothing, we find nothing out. Anna wraps
the blade of the straw knife in two cornstalk leaves and
then sticks the knife in a belt loop so that she looks like
a pirate, Pirate Anna says: The two of us are not going
into the pond, Anna says: Not as long as they stand
beside it watching. Otherwise we do not speak. At the
edge of the woods it is as lonely and silent as always.

The woods are as lonely and silent and black and impenetrably black as always, late at night the fog over the ridge lifts. We stand on the ridge, safely hidden in the darkness behind the first row of corn, our hands in our pants pockets, the straw knife in Pirate Anna's belt-loop, and in each hand a brick. Before us and behind us stands corn, farther back in the valley wheat, the valley lies scarcely ten meters below us, but we call it the valley as always, we call it the valley even though it is not one. Somewhat farther toward the front in the valley stands rye, to the right of it barley, then comes corn and, across the valley as far as the dirt road, wheat again. On the dirt road, parked not far from our house, is a whole row of military cars strung neatly one behind another, on this side of the dirt road stand cabbage and turnips in long rows, carrots, potatoes, and above and around us lie the woods, beginning on the ridge that runs around the fields and our house and Wasznar and Antonina's farm, that encloses the fields and our house and Wasznar and Antonina's farm in a basin, the valley. We build a castle out of bricks and wood. We walk rather clumsily and still have very chubby faces and arms and legs, Marek doesn't smoke yet. He holds Anna on his arm and adjusts Anna's little dress and brushes the sand out of Anna's hair, and gives Anna a pat when she fights with Antonina and gives Anna a pat when she hits Antonina, and pulls at her little arm as if he were her father when she tries to stuff sand into her mouth because the sand is our cake, but he is not her father, he is her brother, and so Anna breaks free, Anna screams: Leave me alone, she screams: You're not my father, screams at least once a day: You're not my father, she says she finds a large pile of bricks in a shed behind Wasznar's house, she says: For our castle, and we also find in the shed behind Wasznar's house an old tea kettle and battered metal curtain rods, we take from Wasznar's kitchen the curtains that Antonina's mother makes out of lace when Antonina is still little, we find a few teabags and a sugar shovel, a set of good silverware and the candelabrum from the piano in the living room that none of us ever sees burning. We bring everything into the castle. We build a castle and set up our castle beautifully, and Marek is the architect and the lord of the castle and the court jester and the rich traveling merchant and the traveling minstrel and the traveling barber-surgeon and the knight and the cook and the guard at the drawbridge and the steward and the best archer and the bravest dueler in the land and the most adventurous adventurer, the king. Antonina is the queen, his wife, before he marries her he must first buy the bride, and for a whole day before he's not allowed to see her, and so he buys the bride, Antonina, and there is much clamor and schnapps goes around by the bottle as he bids awkwardly on Antonina, finally buys Antonina, his bride, from some of Antonina's Jedenew schoolmates after an hour, the last bachelor jokes are made and the money, the proceeds that Antonina brings in for her Jedenew schoolmates, is given to the children. It is very loud and scorching hot all day long on the plot between the two houses, and even in the shade under the poplars between Wasznar and Antonina's farm, Marek and Antonina's new house and the house in which we live, an excessive amount of food and drink is passed around, beer, schnapps and black coffee all day long, and all the guests bring along gifts or food and drink, the Jedenew farmers bring the most. They don't have too far to travel, certainly much less far than our maternal relatives from Ladow or our aunt and her husband and family from Nadice or Antonina's mother's relatives from Julowice or Wasznar's family from Kradejew, all the remaining members of the Wasznar family from the environs of Julowice or our paternal relatives from the region around Boiberice, the Jedenew farmers only have to drive for about a half-hour to reach here, and so, early in the morning on the wedding day, they already haul bags and boxes and casks from their small trucks onto our farm and onto the lawn in front of Wasznar's house, Sapetow brings two pigs that he roasts over a fire in the yard, Kaczmarek brings four huge casks of beer and opens one of them, scarcely does he mount it on the rack that supports it, scarcely can Varta provide enough glasses for the Jedenew farmers' refreshment and a glass each for Wasznar, Father and Marek, we want to drink too, but get only a drop of red wine from one of at least thirty bottles of wine that Sieminski picks out especially for the celebration and fetches up out of his cellars, as he explains proudly, Geniek brings cheese and milk, Dzielski more loaves of bread than a wedding gathering of nearly a hundred people can eat, even if they celebrate for a week, Sobuta sausage and even more meat, Krystowczyk brings in a bag the gifts from the Jedenew farmers for the bridal couple and for the baby, for our niece. Unfortunately, during the celebration we can neither be much concerned with nor be greatly interested in the fact that Marek and Antonina are now actually getting married. We are much too busy throwing rice and sweets at Zygmunt, and also at Father and Wasznar and Katarzyna, as she wants us today, on Marek and Antonina's wedding day, to call her exclusively, Today please not Kacia, as she says, for today she wants to be someone to throw rice and sweets and whole bags full of our homemade confetti at, we don't have time for anything else, says Anna. Marek and Antonina get married toward noon in a church far away, in Kradejew, in Kradejew, says Wasznar, Marek tells us in the clearing, because it's certain no one knows us there. Wasznar looks very proud. He takes Antonina in his arms, he kisses her on the cheek, and tears run down both their faces because Antonina's mother would be so happy to see Antonina get married, again and again before Antonina's mother dies, she takes Antonina by the arms, moves her next to Marek and takes Marek by the hands, says: One thing is certain: You two are getting married. Wasznar lets Antonina go and keeps holding onto her with one hand, and with the other takes our father into his arms, kisses him on the cheek, gradually he takes us all into his arms, again and again and all day long, and again and again and all day long he also tries to kiss us, because that's what's done, as he says, repeats again and again, so as to apologize, and only reluctantly does first Marek let him, and then reluctantly our father too, and then reluctantly we too ultimately let him kiss us, once, twice, left, right, then left again, three times, and ultimately kiss him back and all kiss one another again and again, all morning long in Kradejew and then in the late afternoon too, at home. Marek is all red in the face with pure happiness, and his face is also wet. Again and again he insists that it's only sweat, but he laughs and he cries at the same time, that much is certain, he comes between Antonina and Wasznar in front of our house and they call our father over, and we sit down, seven in number, eight counting Julia in Antonina's belly, as Marek demands, he cries: All eight of us in wedding clothes on the bench in front of our house. Katarzyna, Kacia, as we call her, shoots the photo. We climb into the treehouse and take up with us the bricks from the heap of bricks that is the castle. We kick in the castle inadvertently as we fight, pull one another's hair and scratch one another and fall against the outer walls, Marek sits in the castle as it caves in, and we have to press cornstalk leaves against the wound on the head of the architect, the lord of the castle, the court jester, the rich traveling merchant, the traveling minstrel, the traveling barber-surgeon, the knight, the cook, the guard at the drawbridge, the steward, the best archer, the bravest dueler in the land, the most adventurous adventurer, the king, while we bring him home. At home, Father shaves a large circle around the wound with a razor and then sutures the wound with three stitches and puts an iodine bandage on it. Marek grins because he's so brave. We climb into the treehouse and take up with us the bricks from the heap that, years ago, is the castle, so as to be able to defend ourselves if necessary. The treehouse is in the ninth or tenth row of trees behind the ridge, we can see well from the treehouse, we look across the whole valley to the side of the ridge where the dirt road leads onto the ridge and runs into the street to Jedenew. We look at the two houses and Wasznar's stable, Wasznar's converted former barn that Wasznar converts a few years ago into a third house, into Marek, Antonina and Julia's house, the house of a family, we look at our toolshed. We see the soldiers in clean uniforms walking around in our garden and gesticulating and discussing in their clean, stiff uniforms, we see the Jedenew farmers in their Polish farmer clothes, the Kradejew veterinarian in a black suit in the garden sitting silently in the grass, waiting, or see all nineteen of them waiting, sitting on the narrow wooden dock that leads out into the pond behind the house in the garden behind the house, we see Antonina's bright dress drifting in the middle of the pond, we look away. We stack the bricks carefully beside us and in front of us and behind us and around us and carefully remove the clods of dirt and earthworms. We no longer look up and no longer look out at the Jedenew farmers, the soldiers in the garden of our house, we look at the treehouse floor and look at each other from time to time, we keep our gazes lowered and are wholly occupied with the bricks, we don't say a word, for whole eternities, a thousand years already and longer, the treehouse floor and no one else anymore but us. Anna says without speaking: If we speak, the wind carries our voices into the valley, so we do not speak. We do not speak and do not move, there is nothing to say and there is nothing to do.

We sit in the garden behind the house, Wasznar on the bench against the back of the house, we others on the narrow wooden dock that leads out into the pond. We, that is, little Julia is there, she lies in Antonina's arms or on Wasznar's lap and screams from time to time whenever she wakes up only for a few moments, during the greater part of her first four weeks, the last four weeks, she's asleep. Today she's awake much more often and longer than usual, and so Marek says, whenever she wakes up for only a moment on this evening in the garden behind the house, the last evening, because we talk too loudly or because some wind blows over the pond and through the garden and over us: Perhaps she senses something, and strokes her head. Naturally Antonina is there, Antonina who's much calmer than the two of us. Even though she's scarcely older than we are, she's calmer and talks much less than we do, we can hardly ever hold out longer than a few minutes without singing, laughing, screaming, yelling or chattering away, for as long as we can remember only we are to be heard when we three are together, Antonina almost never. We, on the other hand, all day long without pause, Antonina at most once when she enters the house, when she comes the short way from Wasznar's house, takes off her boots or sandals or shoes, when she shouts Hello from the open front door into the house or: Anybody home, calling us from the front door through the whole house. Only then. We're much louder. Sometimes Antonina is to be heard calling something to Krystowczyk across the yard, a cry of greeting or simply his name whenever Krystowczyk walks along the dirt road to our house or to Wasznar and Antonina's farm or rides his old bike to our house from his farm close to Jedenew because he's bringing by an installment of the money he owes Father, or has to discuss something else with Father or Wasznar, or because he simply wants to drop by, because he wants to bring us a new soda or brand of chocolate or just ordinary candied apples that he finds at the market in Jedenew or Kradejew and buys for us, Antonina knows none of the other Jedenew farmers as well as Krystowczyk, we others also know Krystowczyk best and longest by far of all the Jedenew farmers. Krystowczyk has no family, he runs his farm, a purchase with money on loan for many years from Father, together with a few farmhands, otherwise he lives alone, and so for years Krystowczyk watches over us as often as he can and for years shows up at our house at least once a week to bring us kids something or to help us build the treehouse, repair the sleds for the winter, make kites, sharpen the runners of our skates, stuff the old stuffed bears, put up a swing in the garden, brew our own soda, make knots in ropes that are hard to undo, beat the carpets in our rooms, make waterwheels that we set up in a stream in the woods nearby, saw holes in the frozen pond so that we can fish or at least pretend we're fishing, because there are hardly ever fish in the pond, he helps us build snowmen, chop wood and gather brushwood in the woods, he helps us erect castles in the snow, make so many snowballs that they last a whole year, he says and laughs: You never know how the next winter's going to be, and says: It's better to stock up on snowballs as long as you can, and teaches us to read a compass, repair our bikes, clean our bikes, tighten the spokes, patch the tires, oil the chains, adjust the brakes, he shows us how to make a campfire, pitch a tent, make coffee on the campfire, and shows us how to bake small breads on willow sticks over the campfire, he helps Marek repair Father's car and shows him how to use each of the tools correctly, he often does Antonina's homework. He watches over Antonina more than us because Antonina has no siblings and Zygmunt, who also has no siblings, can nonetheless be with us whenever he wants because he lives in our house, and when we're busy in our rooms with what we have to get done for school, Krystowczyk goes over to Antonina's house when he's there at homework time and helps her with her homework as well as he can, often, says Antonina, she has to do her homework over again when Krystowczyk does it, when Krystowczyk does it, says Antonina, I still sit, after Krystowczyk leaves, for half the evening over my notebooks and books and do the homework over again, this time alone, she laughs, she says: He tries very hard, only he never does the work correctly. Sometimes in the summer Antonina sits under the awning of the house in which she and Wasznar live, and sits in the sun, reads, writes, does arithmetic, and then already sees Krystowczyk from a distance riding or walking along the dirt road to our house and Wasznar and Antonina's farm, sometimes she sits in the kitchen when it's raining or snowing, and so, from the window or from her armchair in the sun, she already calls his name from a distance as soon as she sees him, or calls something in greeting so that all on the farm know he's coming. Otherwise she's never to be heard, we're much louder. Especially Anna. She too is there on this evening, naturally, big Anna, as she loves us to call her, Anna, wild Anna who's angry more often than she laughs, even when it's summer, who screams and rages in disappointment more than she's happy about something, for she hates nothing more, as she says, than to be disappointed, especially in summer, there's nothing I hate more than that, as she says, Anna, who's always everywhere, most especially Anna. Very early in the morning, when it's almost still night, she crouches down beside us, when the four of us, as so often, spend the night in the same room in our house, so as to read with us when we wake up much too early and already read together early in the morning, or lies wide-awake with her back against the wall so as to listen when Antonina shuts her eyes and imagines what happens in our lives, whom we marry, where we move, what's the most wonderful, worst, best, dumbest thing that can happen to us in the future, we anticipate everything, or she sits up so as to listen when it's Father who, before he sets off to work on one of the Jedenew farms, comes into our room at the crack of dawn to see if we're perhaps already awake, he sees that we're long since awake, as always when we all spend the night together in the same room, he finds us at the crack of dawn already lying awake and reading, telling stories or simply lying there because we can't sleep any longer, only, soon thereafter and shortly before we actually have to get up, to fall asleep again after all, and then to sleep until we're almost running late. Until he has to go, he tells us wild, invented stories. Once, when we ask him how he, and so we too, come to be on our farms close to Jedenew in the first place, he tells us a story and claims it's a story of his own experience and tells us this story, his story, in the future too, whenever we ask him this question. Whenever we ask him to tell us, he tells us his story, puts on his storyteller face, says with an exaggeratedly deep voice: If you want, I can tell you a wonderful story of how I take a well-meant burden upon myself that nearly brings me misfortune, and then tells us for a long time of how he once, many years ago, even before he knows our mother, directly after his studies in veterinary medicine, must report to military service in Nadice and ultimately, instead of registering for military service on time, is stuck for several days in a snowstorm and, lost in the middle of the deeply snow-covered South Lithuanian heath, sits on a sleigh beside a coachman who speaks scarcely a word to him and in front of a dead woman lying under a black cover, the wife of an innkeeper at whose inn he stops along the way and whom he faithfully promises to take the woman, whom he doesn't even know well enough to retain her name for longer than a few moments, along with him into the next village. Tells how the coachman and he, scarcely do they leave the innkeeper and his children in their lonely house, lose their way in a snowstorm that breaks out over them, can't find their way again, and not until very much later, how much later he doesn't know exactly, half-frozen, manage to get to safety. Tells how he and the coachman thus nearly die as well, and how he ultimately but by chance and only due to the snowstorm meets our mother. How he finds our farms close to Jedenew, three or four years ago Anna instead of Antonina now takes Zygmunt, scarcely one year old, on her arm every morning for weeks while we lie awake, so as to rock him back and forth until he falls sleep, when we, on the four mattresses that lie beside one another covering the entire floor in our room, wait beside one another all night long for daybreak, tell one another stories and jokes for hours so that Antonina can't fall asleep and so can't have bad dreams about her mother in the Nadice hospital, and during this time we again and again must calm Antonina down, distract her, while she waits for Wasznar, who at this time spends most nights in the Nadice hospital with Antonina's mother. Rarely gets in touch and, when it's snowing heavily, sometimes doesn't come home for four or five days in a row, hardly ever shows his face on the farms, even more rarely at his and Father's practice, who lies down between us when he does return from Nadice early in the morning or when it's still half night, and comes into the room while we, by way of exception, are still asleep, inadvertently wakes up little Zygmunt and puts him to sleep again by softly crooning or humming or even singing one of the many hundred songs that he knows. Then he lies between us and his coat smells of the waiting rooms in the hospital, of chloroform and tobacco, one day he comes back from the Nadice hospital early in the morning for the last time and lies down between us and immediately falls asleep. On the last evening in the garden behind the house Antonina is there too, naturally, and Wasznar is there. At times he has Julia on his arm when Antonina gives her to him, at times Zygmunt, whom he lets pull on his beard, Zygmunt's mother is there, Kacia. She sits somewhat apart in the grass, she draws up her knees as always, crosses her ankles and embraces her legs with her arms, her apron lies beside her in the grass. Kacia says Zygmunt's father disappears right after Zygmunt's birth in the big city of Ladow, as she says, and never returns, she says, she's very happy for Antonina, she shouts to Zygmunt not to pull too hard on Wasznar's beard, and emphasizes how happy she is for Marek. Little Zygmunt doesn't yet quite listen to father recounting what happens in Krystowczyk's kitchen. He sits on the wooden dock between us and tries to touch the water's surface with his hands from the wooden dock. And tries to scrape Marek's cigarette stubs and little pebbles out of the gaps between the planks of the wooden dock, he contemplates everything that he finds, collects it in his pants pockets or throws it into the pond, laughs and claps with glee over the little circles that the cigarette stubs, pebbles, sun-dried flower heads that he finds make in the water, Marek is there. He's the only one still in the water, resting his elbows on the end of the wooden dock from in the water, or the first already dried off and dressed, on the bench beside Wasznar or on the wooden dock beside Antonina who carefully presses some ice on the suture in his eyebrow. A radio sits next to him on the wooden dock. We listen to the latest news about the invasion, we listen to the news and the high, excited voice of the speaker on the one station, the somber, seemingly composed voice of another on another station, listen until far into the evening, more and more quietly, ultimately silently, to the latest news, finally see the Jedenew farmers gathering on the dirt road. On this evening, on the last evening, it is Antonina who says softly: They're coming.

It's morning. Our shirts are clammy, the first thing we smell this morning is Wasznar and Antonina's burning farm. Father wakes us on the last morning, he says: Today's the day, and so the fog rises so high that it completely shrouds the fields, the houses, the ridge, the treehouse, the woods. Father too is there on this evening, on the last evening, he sits on the ground beside us, silently or talking, planning, listens to the radio, then says scarcely anything more for several minutes, only listens and looks up briefly from time to time to check with a glance toward the dirt road if someone is not already coming, the fog is so thick that we can scarcely see each other, Anna's first gesture after she awakes is directed at the rope-ladder. We pull the rope-ladder up to us in the treehouse before we fall asleep, Anna's second gesture is directed at the fog. The rope-ladder lies beside her, between us, where it belongs, the fog is all around her, between us, she stretches her hand far out and stretches it as far as she can into the fog and makes it roughly half a meter, her hand is invisible. Laughing soundlessly we fall into each other's arms on this first morning, in the fog we are safe, and so we lie soundlessly and wait silently for evening and night to come, we lie and doze and listen to Marek's stories as always and hear soft clarinet and accordion music coming from we don't know where. Antonina takes the harmonica out of her pocket and, with Anna's head on her belly, softly plays a song that she hears for the first time when two fiddlers from Nadice play the wedding dance music at the wedding, and so Marek, in the clearing in the field, as Antonina softly plays harmonica, begins to tell us about shooting buzzards. Antonina has fruit and cold chicken, she tears a piece of meat from the wings for each of us, and lets us take the meat from her hands. Anna takes her piece, Marek strokes Antonina's belly and Marek strokes Anna's head, Marek gets the biggest piece, Marek says: Listen closely, and he tells us about shooting buzzards, his story. During the last months he tells us over a hundred times about shooting buzzards, but it's a wonderful story, and it's a wonderful and important story, says Marek, and it's very long. The evening is warm and, in a way that only happens on some very few summer evenings close to Jedenew, golden, we want to be allowed to stay awake and lie in the fields as long as possible, so we gladly listen to Marek's story again even for well over the hundredth time, if by doing so we don't have to go home and to bed, Marek tells us: In autumn it's definite that Antonina is having a baby, and I ask Antonina to marry me. Then I ask Wasznar and both say yes, he laughs: And since Antonina unfortunately wants nothing more than to get married in white in a church, Wasznar decides that the wedding should take place in spring before Julia's birth in white in a church, Wasznar says: If that's what Antonina wants, then you're getting married in a church, whatever the cost, even if to do it we have to cheat a little so you convert on time beforehand. He decides to drive to Julowice to visit Adamczyk, he says Adamczyk can forge papers like no other. We drive together to Julowice to visit Adamczyk and pay Adamczyk a trifle, says Marek, Marek says: And Adamczyk forges my papers. He takes a blank passport form, he takes his camera, which he steals during his time with the Kradejew police, and photographs me a few times from all sides. He takes his typewriter and fills out the passport. He has me sign, and takes an official stamp, which he steals during his time on the Kradejew town council, he gives me the passport. We leave, and Wasznar claps me on the shoulders and is happy as a little boy. He takes the passport from my hand and holds up the passport again and again before his eyes as if he simply can't believe that I now, already and without months of waiting and possibly not converting on time before the wedding and before Julia's birth, am catholic, and he kisses me and hugs me, once, twice, it almost seems like he's even happier than I am. Radiant with joy, he takes me by the arm and drags me to the car and then, hours later in Kradejew, radiant with joy, drags me to the rectory to register Antonina and me with the priest. Wasznar says: If that's what Antonina wants, then you're getting married in a church, whatever the cost, though, says Wasznar in full stride, as quietly as he can, despite the fact that he's getting scarcely any air, the wedding is by no means taking place in the Jedenew church. Wasznar says to me, says Marek: They know you in Jedenew, and would immediately notice your unusually swift conversion, and so Wasznar decides we're getting married in Kradejew instead. He says: In Kradejew no one knows us, in Kradejew no one asks questions, we keep the Jedenew farmers occupied on the farm preparing the celebration during the day on the wedding day, it's all the same to the Jedenew farmers where you get married. Marek takes a short break. He stops hammering because it's long since too dark to keep working, somewhere in the twilight he drops his nails onto the treehouse floor, and somewhere in the semidarkness he lays aside his hammer, blows into his hands, which are red from the sudden evening cold, and lies down in the evening cold on his back. We others too toss aside our hammers and nails, lie down like Marek on our backs and lie beside one another in the half-finished treehouse under the cold red autumn sky and stand up and climb carefully down the rope-ladder one after another when Kacia, from the house, from the door that leads out of the kitchen into the garden, calls us to dinner. We climb down, we go into the house and throw our jackets onto the first chair we come across, and to ensure that the treehouse is finished before winter begins, we arrange during dinner, our faces hot with excitement, to go back to the treehouse the next day, to finish building the treehouse, to put up the roof, to put in the door, the windows, the next day we get up at the crack of dawn and get dressed and wash as quickly as we can, and comb each other's hair and braid each other's hair and tie on each other's headscarves and want to rush outside, outside it's snowing. We lie on our bellies, scarcely dare to breathe, and lay aside the rusty hammers and nails as quietly as possible, we look across to our house and see that some of the soldiers are gathering before our house to receive before our house the first of the slowly approaching black trucks. Anna finds an old handkerchief in the treehouse, wipes the rust stains from her hands. For a long time she contemplates the wooden hammer handle. After lying already for half a summer in the still roofless treehouse it's cracked from the sun, since our last time working on the treehouse in November it swells up with rainwater, and after lying already for almost a year altogether in one and the same place in the treehouse it actually scarcely looks like a hammer handle anymore, says Anna, after nearly a year by now in one and the same place in the treehouse it looks like a sponge, and it's spring, the snow is melting, it's two weeks since Purim when Anna asks Marek: Can we finish building the treehouse now. Shaking his head, Marek takes her aside, puts his arm around her and pulls her onto his lap in his rocking chair. Anna smiles, uncertain if he's only kidding when he says: I'm getting married. He says: I can't build treehouses anymore, incredulously and uncertainly smiling, Anna whispers that Marek promises though, last November after it starts snowing: In spring we can continue building, that he proclaims: Help clean the house, help Kacia bake what there is to bake, then you have something to do while it's snowing, she says Marek promises: In spring after Purim we can continue building. We can build the missing roof and finally, finally put in the missing door and the missing windows, he promises: That shouldn't even take us a day, Anna says: It's a good two weeks since Purim, in a few days the snow's going to melt, it's long since warm enough, but Marek doesn't respond, he repeats: I'm getting married. Anna lies on her back in the treehouse, the hammer in her hand, without speaking she says all this completely serves us right. After Purim the two of us must finish building the treehouse alone so that we're now dry and warm in the treehouse and also don't have to be all too careful, she says, if at least the two of us return to the treehouse in spring after Purim, if necessary the two of us alone, without Marek and Antonina, to finish building the treehouse, then we now have a roof and outer walls made of tarpaper and pressboard, if the two of us conceal the treehouse even better in the tree after Purim, then we're now warm and dry for an indefinite time, never can anyone find us here, not during the day, especially not at night. Not even when the fog lifts for a long time, only why do the two of us not return to the treehouse alone in spring. Anna lies on her back, the hammer in her hand, her head on her stack of bricks, without waiting for a reply she falls asleep. Marek gives her a pat on the shoulders, he takes her head from the pillow, he says: We have to go, he dries her face and makes her get up, he leaves, on his way out he says: Calm down, and leaves. Marek, with his twenty years, is only a few years older than Antonina and we are, but he's already long since a man. He smokes and can fix up cars and last winter he begins working on weekends as Father and Wasznar's assistant in Father and Wasznar's practice, gathering experience that he needs if he one day takes over the practice. Suddenly he's already earning money. We're still going to school. We want to build treehouses. We set dolls on the window ledges of our rooms and braid each other's hair and braid our dolls' hair and sew them little dresses. We make wreaths out of the flowers that we pick from the fields in summer. Marek works and already earns money, nothing pleases him more, as he says, than earning money, except Antonina naturally, as he says, and except little Julia naturally, his daughter, our niece, and except the two of us naturally, as he says, as for us, on the other hand, even still today scarcely anything pleases us more than, during spring vacation, early in the morning amid the chirping of birds, walking again through the fields to Jedenew for the first time after the snow melts, then buying in Jedenew everything that neither we store in our pantry nor Wasznar and Antonina in theirs, buying in Jedenew as much as we can carry of all those things that run out during the last winter weeks. Father writes down what we need, Kacia adds something, we start walking every morning at six toward Jedenew, at half-past nine we're there, and we buy canned food, rice and oil, soap, combs, barrettes, school notebooks and yeast, we buy much more, we walk to Jedenew every morning during the first two spring vacation weeks, while Father and Wasznar and, as of recently, Marek too, are on their way

45

CLOSE TO JEDENEW

by car to take care of sick pigs and injured horses on the nearby Jedenew farms, we walk to Jedenew because that's what we do for years already and because it's the most wonderful thing of all to do in the first vacation days and because we four, the two of us and Marek and Antonina, walk together to Jedenew every morning during every vacation until now, and so we decide that at least the two of us are going to carry on walking to Jedenew every morning during every vacation as always, if necessary without Marek and Antonina from now on, no one but the two of us. Marek says: We have to go to work, and when he gets up to go Anna flings herself back onto her bed, she says into the pillow: No reason to worry. It's scarcely three months ago that Mister Marek is not yet a doctor. That Mister Marek still loves to build treehouses just as much as we do. She says: But it's amazing how much can change in only three months, isn't it. She presses her face into her pillow, she sobs softly. She sits down on the windowsill and suddenly jumps up and screams into Antonina's face: If you two wouldn't get such a dumb idea, everything here would be as always forever, she falls back onto her bed, remains lying, loudly sobbing. She wakes up from the heavy engine noise of the fire truck driving up. She gets up, and we watch from the treehouse as the soldiers begin to extinguish the flames of the little that remains of Wasznar's burning farm, presumably so that the fire doesn't spread to the woods and to our house, which they still need, Anna says: Amazing how much can change in only a few moments, isn't it. She says: It's scarcely a handful of moments ago that we're still sitting together on the wooden dock behind the house, reading, swimming, drinking summer punch, that our wooden dock is still our wooden dock and our house is still our house, she says: And now we watch as they try to extinguish the flames of Wasznar and Antonina's farm and empty out our house, we watch as Antonina jumps up and Marek tries to hold her back before she can run out of the room. It's evening. From the treehouse we watch as night falls over the fields and over our house, after the chicken Antonina gives us some fruit. We bring along cold potato salad into the field and raspberry soda, we bring along chocolate into the field and, in a porcelain bowl, pudding that Katarzyna, Kacia as we call her, cooks for us, and Antonina passes out the fruit, and we pass out potato salad, raspberry soda, chocolate, pudding, while Marek tells his story, he tells us: Naturally the priest in Kradejew doesn't know me. He knows Wasznar, at least by sight, because our house and Wasznar and Antonina's farm belong to the Jedenew administrative unit and Jedenew, though it's so far away from Kradejew that the Kradejew priest probably doesn't even know that Jedenew, let alone any place close to Jedenew, exists, belongs to the parish of the Kradejew diocese, so the priest, in all the years that he is now already priest in Kradejew, inevitably crosses paths with Wasznar from time to time: When Wasznar notifies him almost twenty years ago of his own wedding and three or four years later of Antonina's baptism, then three or four years ago of the death of Antonina's mother, and over the years at least once or twice a year when Wasznar, in the first years still just with Antonina's mother, then later together with Antonina's mother and little Antonina, today with only Antonina, goes to the service on Saturday evening not as usual in the Jedenew church, but rather by way of exception in the Kradejew church, because by chance he's staying in Kradejew at the moment to buy equipment, syringes, medicines for Father and Wasznar's practice, or on Sunday when, after such purchases, he stays overnight in Kradejew by way of exception, because it's raining or storming too heavily to drive the long way back home on Saturday evening, stays the night in Kradejew in a hotel or in a boardinghouse, then attends the Kradejew early service on Sunday. So the priest, after all the years, at least knows Wasznar's face. Perhaps he can't always and all the time immediately put a name to Wasznar's face when he sees him a few times a year in his church and also runs into him sometime every few years outside of the Kradejew church, at the Kradejew market, in a Kradejew restaurant, and yet he recognizes him and greets him those few times a year that he sees him when Wasznar, on Saturday evening or Sunday morning, leaves the church after the service, greets him amiably also whenever he meets him sometime every few years outside of the Kradejew church. Me, on the other hand, he naturally knows not at all, says Marek, he says: And so Wasznar begins, when the priest appears suspicious from the first moment on, to tell the priest a story, my story. According to Adamczyk's false passport I come into the world not close to Jedenew but rather in Ladow. The passport has me already converting when I'm scarcely of age, and it has me converting in Ladow so that, Wasznar explains later, the priest doesn't even think to inquire about me in Jedenew, and in Ladow, says Wasznar, in Ladow no one keeps sufficient track of the over one-and-a-half million files, in Ladow, says Wasznar, in Ladow the priest is not going to inquire. According to the passport, says Marek, I finish my schooldays in Ladow, Wasznar claims before the priest that Antonina and I first meet when Antonina visits her aunt, Wasznar's sister who's married to a man in Ladow, after the death of her mother, on the street, in a coffeehouse, in a shop, he no longer recalls where exactly, somewhere in Ladow, he says, we become friends immediately on that Ladow street, in that Ladow coffeehouse, wherever, as Wasznar formulates it before the Kradejew priest, he says that Antonina stays with her aunt in Ladow for a few more months, during which he himself visits Ladow too, so as to meet me, and after the wedding I'm moving in with Wasznar together with Antonina on Wasznar and Antonina's farm close to Jedenew so as to work there for the Jedenew farmers as his and Father's assistant, so as to take over the practice sometime later after my studies. He says Antonina and I are moving into his former barn, he says: Luckily I'm already converting my former barn for a few years into a house for my daughter Antonina and her family should she one day have one, he says: Now the day is here, he says: And though the Jedenew church is considerably nearer, we'd like to have the wedding here in the Kradejew church because the Kradejew church is much larger and more spacious, the Jedenew church on the other hand not much more than a large chapel. The Kradejew church offers ample space for a wedding as large as ours, he says: Just think of Marek's maternal relatives from Ladow, plus the relatives of his aunt and of his aunt's husband from Nadice or the relatives of my late wife from Julowice or all my family from Kradejew, all the rest of our relatives from the environs of Julowice or also Marek's paternal relatives from the region around Boiberice, and Wasznar is not satisfied until the priest appears convinced or at least no longer asks questions, nods so that the little wrinkles under his chin jiggle, and with thin, spear-pointed fingers, the priest, while he scrutinizes us intently from above, riffles through the pages of a Bible lying before him on the lectern, without looking he finds what he's searching for, taps with his endless spear-fingers on a passage without looking, and while he stares at us, Wasznar and me, he reads without looking, keeping his eyes on us, following the text with his finger: I will give peace in your land, asks: How does that please you. He proposes a date and sees us off. And with his endlessly long knitting-needle-fingers the priest, during his sermon a good half a year later, riffles through the pages of a Bible that lies before him, between him and Antonina and me, on a lectern before the altar, finally finds what he's searching for, taps on a passage without looking, reads without looking and concludes the mass during which he marries us, Antonina and me, reads: I will give peace in your land, and you shall sleep, and none shall make you afraid. I will rid your land of savage beasts, and no sword shall go through your land. Marek says not until today, here, does he truly comprehend what Wasznar does for him, for them both, for Antonina and him, he says, probably he can hardly ever thank him, Wasznar, enough. Not until the second or third day do we notice how hungry we are. We draw lots, and Anna has to set off first to scrape up something to eat in the fields, we agree that she should go as soon as it's dark enough and the fog is high enough that she can climb without risk out of the treehouse, down the rope-ladder and onto the ridge to fetch what we need from the fields. Before she goes, we wait until the guard in the garden behind the house is alone and turns away from the ridge and from the woods, when she goes, Marek gazes silently after Antonina, gazes silently at the wall for a few minutes, and then says to Anna: I have to go to work, and Marek, already on his way out, turns around briefly once more outside the bedroom door, and says with a smile: In summer then, in summer, when Zygmunt is big enough to get something out of it too, we can finish building the treehouse. He asks: What do you two think of that. Only a few moments later we see from the window Marek climbing onto the box of our sleigh beside father. The sleigh's tracks, after father's, are the second set in the fresh snow, which falls once again unexpectedly overnight but is finally the last snowfall of this winter, from the window we see, scarcely does the sleigh leave the farm, Antonina too leaving the house and striding through the garden, through the gap in the leafless, brown bushes between the poplars to Wasznar's farm. Her tracks are the third set this morning, Anna flings open the window, cries: I'm sorry, and we wait, and leave the window open while we wait, and wipe the snow lying on the windowsill from the windowsill so that it snows while we wait, Anna says: She's not coming back, and Antonina does not come back, Anna says: And so Mister Marek is going to work now to earn money for his family, for he's getting married soon. At the window Anna says: Mister Marek is getting married soon, she says: I can already foresee now what happens next. First they get married. Then Mister Marek keeps working for a while for Father and Wasznar and earns money for a while, setting aside a little of it so as to go together with Antonina afterward to Ladow, to study veterinary medicine for a few years in Ladow, and then he comes back someday when the two of us are still sitting here, together with Wasznar and Zygmunt and Father, and Kacia too is still here when they come back, during the whole time that Marek and Antonina are in Ladow we're all nowhere else but here. Perhaps in Jedenew from time to time to go shopping during vacation but that's all, she says: They come back from Ladow, and we're here. She says: They come back from Ladow after they see and do things in Ladow that are inconceivable here, while we here do the same as always in the same way as always, they on the other hand now do nothing but utterly different things than we do here, and do everything utterly differently than we do, she says: But we'd probably never want things any different, would we, she says: If they even do ever come back, and so we get up slowly one after the other, go down the stairs one after the other as always from the second floor of our house to the ground floor, very slowly or raging wild or yelling or singing or laughing or simply silent, and go through the hallway and go through the living room one after the other as always and come to Kacia in the kitchen at her counter. Help her bake Christmas cookies for another whole winter day, as always.

It's very early in the morning, almost still night, when, only a few weeks after I finish my studies, I leave the house to report to military service in Nadice, says Father, when he tells the story, his story, he tells it and, at the sight of our faces that, even after we already hear this story so often and even after we already long since know that this story never takes place as he recounts it to us, are still so raptly attentive, he cannot but laugh loudly again and again so that Anna, laughing as well and yet, even after all the years, still listening just as spellbound as we others, says: Don't believe a word he says, you can't believe a single word he says, and Father says: No, believe me, and tells us: A sleigh that I hire for the trip to Nadice waits in front of the house on this morning, a flat, open sleigh with a small cargo area behind the coach box. It's windless, it's snowing only very lightly, it's still quite dark, and I light my way with a lantern through the ankle-deep snow to the sleigh. I bring along a knapsack with provisions and clothing and a blanket, the man on the box gives me a nod, he appears to have with him nothing more than his pipe, a few pillows and blankets, a small knapsack under the coach box. The horse snorts as I approach, the coachman nods, softly mumbles a word of greeting, or perhaps only nods and doesn't mumble at all, not even so much as that, and so is silent, smokes his pipe and sets off, scarcely do I sit down. And perhaps, on this ice-cold, dark morning, it's nothing but the cold or the weariness, the disquiet in the face of the long day and the impending military stint in Nadice, the nervous excitement, that makes me think during the first stretch of the way exclusively about whether the coachman didn't perhaps say something after all, that even makes me believe after a good half hour of reflection that I do in fact hear him say something when I sit down beside him, perhaps, I think after a good stretch of the way, he does in fact say something, I'm not sure, but ultimately I believe I truly hear him saying, mumbling: A white horse. And sitting beside him on the box, I hear him saying, without taking the pipe out of his mouth, or rather: I believe, after I thoroughly talk myself into it, that I hear him, hear him in truth perhaps not at all, as he observes the freezing horse only slowly getting moving through the snow that reaches up to its knees, softly saying: My horse is injured, and I must borrow this horse, a white horse, says the coachman, perhaps. And white horses, he says, white horses only seldom mean something good, I imagine and talk myself into believing he says to me, we set off. In our house the light goes out, from out of another comes Caslaw with a large snow shovel, in front of a third work is already underway, and another sleigh comes toward us picking up a few children from the houses to bring them to school in the neighboring village. We pass beyond the edge of the village, the last houses, before us the slowly but steadily lifting darkness and the street clearly discernible between the trees, the snow crunches under the runners, the wind dies away completely, I don't want to worry all too much about what the coachman perhaps says or perhaps not, I soon fall asleep, and one of the soldiers sits in a living room armchair beside the door that leads out of the kitchen into the garden and to the pond behind the house, appears to sleep as well, doesn't stir. In the house and in the garden, by the pond, on the dirt road, in our treehouse, it is silent, Anna sleeps with her back to Wasznar and Antonina's smoldering farm, Father says: On the first evening we decide to sleep at an inn that we find along the way at the edge of the woods, we stop. So begins Father's story. And so begins one among many of ours: On a school day last autumn or the autumn before it rains all day long, and while the old priest teaches the others in the school building, five or six of us stand, as always when the priest is teaching, in the schoolyard in front of the school, and for quite a while we, in the rain and in the cold, still in short and thin late summer clothes, jump rope or play hopscotch until the priest ultimately calls us in to join the others after all. He has us spread out our things, steaming in the warm classroom, on the stove and lay them on the floor in front of the stove, and has us sit down behind him in the heap of brushwood with our backs toward the stove and with our faces, glowing red within a few moments from the stove, directed toward the class so as to listen to what he reads to the others, we may say nothing, he says, we must be silent, as he says, and may participate in his lesson only by way of exception, and may tell no one, as he impresses upon both us and the others in the classroom several times, that we're participating and are even allowed to participate in his lesson, but only by way of exception, as he says and repeats several times with a stern face, only by way of exception, he says, and: Solely because the weather's suddenly so bad. We must be even quieter than the others, as he says, but we may stay nonetheless, he says, as long as it's raining, and reads to the others of Ephraim and of Jephthah's Gileadites, the stove rattles and seethes and pumps persistently away, the priest reads very softly, and it smells only faintly of alcohol from the rattling stove, the classroom smells of burning and burnt wood as always and of the still fresh heap of brushwood in front of the stove and the already burning brushwood that we sometimes collect behind the church in the middle of Jedenew when the teacher asks us to, when one of our grades is not yet final, when it's dry enough for a few days in a row, the firewood supply in the school scarce and the next weekly firewood delivery still a few days away, and the priest reads to the others of the war of the Ephraimites against Jephthah, we may be present nonetheless. He reads of the battle by the Jordan and of the fugitives of Ephraim, for Gilead lies between Ephraim and Manasseh, and because Ephraim is in the wrong and wants to battle, though Jephthah doesn't know and can't find out why, the Gileadites battle against the Ephraimites and occupy the fords of the Jordan that lead across to Ephraim before Ephraim can occupy them, and they defeat Ephraim and its soldiers, and when one of the defeated Ephraimites wants to flee from the land of Gilead back to Ephraim, the Gileadites ask him by the ford of the Jordan where he's from, and make him say shibboleth if he claims not to be an Ephraimite, and cast him into the Jordan if he doesn't pronounce shibboleth right, because it's well-known everywhere and everyone knows that none of the Ephraimites can pronounce shibboleth right, so that there fall at that time of Ephraim forty and two thousand, forty and two thousand, reads the priest and repeats the number and wrinkles his forehead, reading the story of Jephthah and Ephraim once more to himself and then leafing through the stories of Ibzan and Elon and Abdon and Samson until the hour is over and it's afternoon so the priest sends us all out into the rain to go home. We too have a shibboleth. We agree on a sign with which Anna is to announce her return: A thrush's whistle, two soft strikes against the tree trunk below the treehouse with a block of wood left over from building the treehouse, lying on the ground in the woods under the ferns. We agree, at the sound of the whistle, the strikes, to check through the still open door-hole of the treehouse and see who's standing below before we react to the whistle, to the strikes, we agree not to lower the rope-ladder until we're sure that it is in fact the other standing below, we agree to dance through the woods when it's all over, like Marek and Antonina in the days before and after their wedding, when it's all over, Marek in the field, in the circle mowed in the field, holds Antonina in his arms, says, whispers: Tonight we dance through the fields, and make a hoist out of a rotten piece of rope still lying in the treehouse from making the rope-ladder, out of a board, wedge the rope through a crack in the board, knot the rope under the board and then lower the board on the rope carefully to the other standing below so that she can lay on the board what she scrapes up in the fields at night. We pull the hoist into the treehouse, we have to pull a few times because we can lay only two things at a time on the board so as to maintain the balance of the hoist, we pull the hoist again and again up into the treehouse and lower the hoist again and again out of the treehouse to the one standing below, when everything is up above the other follows on the rope-ladder. We agree to take turns going into the fields, the first time the one, the second time the other, the third time the one, the fourth time the other, no matter what we want to go at least twice a night, the one time the one, the other time the other, the next time the one, the time after next the other, so as to gather in the field all that we need in the treehouse. Toward the front of the pantry we find one evening a bag half-full of small, dry wheat rolls that Kacia keeps for bread-crumb coating and for the birds, Marek takes the bag, to the left in the pantry we find a bag half-full of wrinkly red apples that Kacia keeps for cakes, compote and for the birds, Antonina takes the bag. All the way in the back of the pantry sits a jug half-full with thick sunflower oil, Anna takes the jug, we take Zygmunt by the hands between us and creep out of the pantry into the kitchen and through the kitchen and through the back door out into the garden, up into the half-finished treehouse, it's early autumn. It's summer, end of June, we're going to fight, says Anna, Pirate Anna, but we need to be careful. We agree not to stay away longer than necessary when we go to procure something to eat from the fields, and never to take even the slightest risk when we go. Never to cross the dirt road and by no means to try to find Zygmunt, not to try to find out what's become of Marek, and not to try to get to father's car on the dirt road for whatever reason. Not to try to play the heroine. We agree not to search for a possible escape route when we go, not to try to get closer to our house, not to try to find out what exactly is going on in our house, we arrange to get something to eat from the fields and to return to the treehouse as quickly and quietly as possible. When Marek and Father return from their rounds of the Jedenew farmers' farms, we sit together in the living room. We arrange with Marek to wallpaper the still half-finished treehouse once it's finished, and to set up the currently half-finished treehouse, once it's finished, like a real house, like our castle, we arrange to fetch the old tea kettle from the castle, which caves in years ago, and to fetch the battered metal curtain rods, the curtains, wash them, iron them, fold them up and save them until the treehouse is finished. We arrange to ask Kacia to give us one or two handfuls of new curtain rings, we want to take teabags from our kitchen and a container of water, a sugar shovel, we fetch the wheat rolls, the dry apples, the sunflower oil from the pantry, and fetch from the kitchen a set of silverware that we no longer need in the house, for our kitchen in the treehouse. The candelabrum that stands for years on the piano in the living room without anyone ever seeing it burning, the candelabrum, says Marek, he says, it's fine if we take it now, in summer, into the treehouse, and then later, in late autumn, toward the beginning of winter, says Marek, the candelabrum at least must go back in the house, while all the other things may remain in the treehouse. Never, says Marek with his arms crossed over his chest, never is he going to part with the candelabrum, and he says that, says Marek, even though not even he, who's the oldest among us by a few years, can remember ever seeing the candelabrum burning, Marek says: The candelabrum stands on the piano with the same unlit candles, the same dust on its arms since always, he says: As long as I can remember, Marek says: And on the piano it shall stand in the future too. He says: With the exception of those few months that it spends in our treehouse during the summer, we arrange to work daily on the treehouse through the whole summer, to start on the outside of the treehouse, cover it with tarpaper, line it with pressboard, then to set it up, Marek says: So that the treehouse is finished before Antonina and I go to Ladow in autumn. He says: The candelabrum has its place on the piano, it can stand in the treehouse temporarily, the treehouse is just as good a place for the candelabrum as the piano, at the very most perhaps the candelabrum may stand someday on another, new piano, but certainly its place is forever on a piano and forever on a piano within our family. Nowhere else. We look at each other, we suspect for days already that Marek's going to say to us what he now says to us, but now we don't know what he's talking about, he says: And when the candelabrum isn't in the treehouse, it stands on a piano within our family, no matter whether it stands on this old piano here in the house or on another, new piano in another house of the family. In my house, for example, in which a new piano shall stand in the living room, he says: The living room is over there in Wasznar's former barn, he says, if we have no objection, in autumn, when the candelabrum is of no use to anyone in the treehouse over the winter anyway, he wants to fetch the candelabrum from the treehouse and take it with him to Ladow over the winter, then, in Ladow, place it on a living room wall unit in his and Antonina's Ladow apartment, then, during the next few years, take the candelabrum out of the treehouse before each winter and take it with him to the Ladow apartment over the winter, then, in a few years, after his return from Ladow, place the candelabrum once and for all on a new piano in his house over there in Wasznar's former barn, leave it standing there unlit, as always, a remembrance. We sit speechlessly beside each other on Kacia's counter in the kitchen or sit beside each other on the velvet-covered armchair, it can't, says Marek, do even us two much good anymore in a few years to have a candelabrum in the treehouse, and we sit speechlessly beside each other in complete surprise on the window ledge opposite Marek, with our backs against the ice-cold, steamed-up windowpane, and can't believe any of what Marek tells us, we jump from Kacia's counter in the kitchen or from the arms of the armchair or from the window ledge onto the floor, without listening further to Marek and, even though we already suspect for days what now comes, without understanding even one word of what Marek tells us. We know for days already how it's coming, namely just as it now comes, but for days we're convinced that we're imagining mixed-up things, fantasizing as we always do, at sixteen we still braid every day the hair of our dolls that we arrange on the window ledges, and tell each other fairy tales, there's nothing we'd rather do. We make up stories, everything that happens at our home close to Jedenew is a story, and when nothing happens, we make something up. Here in the treehouse we don't know which of the many stories that we tell each other in the treehouse while Wasznar and Antonina's farm burns, which of these stories that we tell because they actually happen or because we only make them up, sell them to ourselves as our stories because we for a few moments can't remember what really happens, which story is true and which false, we decide it doesn't matter to us, sitting in the treehouse we remember or invent just anything, we braid each other's hair and perhaps invent our story so as to be able to tell it, but perhaps not. Even Marek's and our future is a story, this story: Marek lives forever at our home, together with us, with Father and Katarzyna, Kacia, as we call her, and Zygmunt in our house close to Jedenew, Wasznar and Antonina live together forever on Wasznar and Antonina's farm, over there, on the other side of the poplars, on their farm close to Jedenew, we walk to Wasznar and Antonina's farm through the dense poplars, across a strip of meadow to Wasznar and Antonina's farm, but by no means does Marek ever live together with Antonina, without us, in Ladow or elsewhere, especially not here at our home close to Jedenew in Wasznar's former barn, without us. For days and weeks, ever since Marek and Antonina decide to get married, we foresee, but never think about it, that Marek wants to buy himself his own piano, a piano for his own house, while in our house a beautiful old piano stands in the living room, Father's piano. We snub him while Marek speaks, we turn away while Marek speaks, standing with our backs to him we give him the silent treatment, and Marek explains angrily: We're going to Ladow to study, he says: Next autumn, he turns around and disappears, it's already almost morning when Anna finally returns to the treehouse, she apologizes, she says she gets lost in the fields, and when she sits in the treehouse she realizes: After all, for years and years we don't go into the fields a single time during the summer in total darkness. One after another, after each lowering of the hoist from the treehouse, she lays the things that she brings with her from the fields onto the hoist. She lays a half-dozen corncobs, ten carrots and a head of cabbage from her apron onto the hoist as quietly as possible, she climbs without a sound up the lowered rope-ladder into the treehouse as soon as everything is up above, when she sits in the treehouse she says: It's already late, already almost morning, we might as well only go once tonight. We each take a corncob and two carrots, we hold the head of cabbage out of the treehouse when it begins to rain a little toward sunrise, so as to wash the dirt and earthworms from the head of cabbage in the warm summer rain, we peel leaf after leaf from the head of cabbage, and chew on them for a long time. We fall asleep back to back when it's long since daylight, almost noon, we sit upright and still tense with our backs against the inner walls of the treehouse, we observe carefully from the treehouse as, at the door that leads from the garden into the kitchen of our house, ultimately also in the house and in the garden around our house, things gradually begin to stir. The soldier stands up from our living room armchair and stretches and, with his arms stretched far out before him, looks for an endlessly long time in our direction, and looks so directly toward our treehouse that it seems impossible that he could ever turn away and look elsewhere, finally he turns away, looks elsewhere, without discovering the treehouse, someone finally relieves him and he goes into the house, stretching, his replacement sits down in the living room armchair, dozes. And so Zygmunt, yawning, lays his head beside Anna's head on Antonina's belly, Antonina's stroking hand on his nape, he says in a few childish words: The baby's walking through your belly, he laughs, and Marek tells us about shooting buzzards, Marek's story: In October, soon after Wasznar and I return from the Kradejew rectory, the leadership of the Nadice garrison changes. In December I ask the new commandant for a week off in spring for the wedding in Kradejew and for my enrollment at the university in Ladow, I say: My weekend off doesn't suffice for that, I explain to the commandant that I already ask his predecessor, who thinks very highly of me, for this week off, his predecessor assents. I'm lying, naturally, and naturally the commandant can't find the necessary documents anywhere, they don't exist, he says he wants to think it over. In January and February he sends me out of his office four or five times without comment after I knock, after a soldier on guard opens in response to my knocking, after I present my request anew to the commandant in his office. At the beginning of March I address the commandant during one of his tours of inspection through the dormitories of the barracks when he checks my bed and the area around my bed for order and cleanliness, he does not reply. At the end of March, a few days before I tell you two in your room for the first time of our Ladow plans, Father and Wasznar and Antonina and I are already considering postponing the wedding, we celebrate the commandant's birthday in the meeting hall of the barracks. Very late at night, on my way back to my barrack, I find the commandant alone, leaning on a watchtower, drunk and singing some song in a low voice and very cheerful, and scarcely do I stand for a few moments beside him when he, already laughing, takes me into his arms, I begin to sing along with him. Singing, arm in arm, we stagger up the stairs into the watchtower. Up above he suddenly lets go of me, snatches the rifle from the hands of the soldier on guard and sends him with a wave of the hand down the stairs, cries: We're taking over. Steps to the railing of the platform, leans on the railing, falls silent. The watchtower stands at the western edge of the Nadice garrison, and a good day's walk northeast from the garrison through the woods leads to Wasznar and Antonina's farm and to our house close to Jedenew, And to our treehouse, Anna interjects, and Marek says: And to our treehouse, he says: The commandant stands at the railing, leans on the railing, the rifle stands beside him, and he looks over the woods before us, below the watchtower: nothing but woods, at the far end, on the other side of the woods: our farm, the treehouse and the sunrise. The commandant looks for a long time into the dawn without stirring, I stand somewhat indecisively beside him. I don't quite know what I'm supposed to do: Go, stay, say something, be silent, I decide not to go, to stay, to say nothing, I'm silent and want to stay so as to take the first opportunity to ask once again about my week off, I think: Now just don't make a mistake, and so I stand behind my commandant and wait behind my commandant for an endlessly long time, for what I don't quite know, presumably for him to stir, and while I wait, I wonder, while I stand, whether he's not perhaps already long since asleep. He's not asleep. He stirs a little, his back jerks, he straightens up without turning around, he looks from the watchtower down over the woods and looks beyond the woods toward the rising sun, he says: At home I go buzzard hunting each spring, he says: So you want your week off, he says: Each spring, scarcely is it spring and finally somewhat drier, the snow melts, I take my rifle on my days off. I go buzzard hunting with my son or with one of my sons-in-law, he turns around to me, he says: I'd like to shoot buzzards now, wouldn't you. We teach each other to speak to each other without saying anything, we teach ourselves to speak by writing in the air, we give each other signs and laugh or just nod to each other, which by itself means a lot. Marek helps us. He knows the system inside out, and because we, especially during the day, must not make the slightest noise, because Anna in the treehouse repeatedly, again and again, says: If we speak, the wind carries our voices down into the valley, across to our house, we speak soundlessly to each other by sitting opposite each other and forming with our fingers the letters of what we have to say to each other without delay, as we believe. Marek takes a piece of paper and scrawls the alphabet in childish handwriting on the paper, then explains to us the form of every single letter for several minutes, though naturally we already know the letters well enough for years, but Marek believes that just because he's a few years older than we are, we're still kids and don't yet know or understand anything at all, let alone know or understand anything, be it only the letters, as well as he does or even better, and so he lets nothing stop him from explaining to us how to form the letters of the alphabet with our fingers, shows us for every single letter of the alphabet how it must be formed with the fingers if others are to understand. He demonstrates to us every single letter one after another, forms the letters with his fingers, we imitate him, form the letters of the alphabet with our fingers and then speak to each other for almost two weeks exclusively in this way, with our fingers and without speaking. And for almost two weeks it's silent upstairs in the house. Upstairs in the house our rooms are next to each other, upstairs in the house it's otherwise almost never silent, silent at the very most at night, but even then only very rarely, says Father sometimes, naturally only kidding, now for two whole weeks even upstairs in the house it's constantly, very unusually silent, Father says: As otherwise only in the graveyard. For almost two weeks we talk exclusively with our fingers, we no longer scream at each other when we quarrel, we no longer scream anything to each other from one room to the other when we want something from each other, now we get up and go over into the other's room when we want something from her so as to signify to her with our fingers what it is that we want, now we get up and go over into the other's room when there's something left to quarrel over from the morning or from the day before or from the week before, we no longer scream, now we scream soundlessly, stand before each other and give each other signs. For two whole weeks it's completely silent upstairs in the house, and several times a day Father audibly breathes sighs of relief, he makes jokes about us and pretends he doesn't see us when we're standing in front of him, because, as he says, we actually immediately cease to exist as soon as we're only once briefly silent, he laughs and Kacia too is happy about the so unaccustomed silence. Kacia so enjoys listening to the radio while working, as she cooks or irons or sews or embroiders or cleans or washes or scrubs or sweeps, and for almost two weeks she can listen to the radio while working as she pleases, because we utter not a single word as long as it's not absolutely necessary. With our fingers we speak about all sorts of things. We communicate to each other what we want to play the next day, a Sunday, when we're off school, and communicate to each other what assignments we have to get done for school the next day. We communicate to each other where exactly in the kitchen or pantry or where in the stairwell or where else in the house Kacia hides sweets, cakes or whatever else we're not supposed to find from us, we're in agreement: If we speak, the wind carries our voices into the valley and into our garden behind our house, so we do not speak, and communicate to each other solely with our fingers what we'd like from the fields when it's the other's turn to go at night to get something to eat from the fields. We ask for chicken from the fields in fun, and write it to the other with our fingers in the air, we ask for cooked peas, thick meat soup, Kacia's potato dumplings, we write and write: apple compote, vegetable soup, red cabbage, we write and we communicate to each other what we suppose is happening with our house over there in the fog and with our garden, with our pond and with our fields, wonder whether they're already long since searching for us or whether they even realize that we're missing, the two of us. Communicate to each other that Krystowczyk surely notices our absence, he knows the family, he's aware we're missing, he knows us well enough to realize immediately that we're not there, Krystowczyk most surely notices our absence, we wonder where, if not long since among them, little Zygmunt may be at the moment. Wonder with our fingers what we're to do once it really begins to rain, we sit in our bathing suits in the roofless treehouse and hold boards that are left over from building the treehouse over our heads when it begins to drizzle or to rain, when it's dry, and when we don't have to hold on to anything, we speak with our fingers about what's going to happen with us. Anna, Pirate Anna, says without speaking: We're going to fight, just wait and see, and Marek tells us about shooting buzzards, his story.

In a small inn in the middle of the South Lithuanian heath, which is traversable only with difficulty for weeks already, where we decide to spend the first night, the innkeeper's wife lies for three days in a small room behind the barroom under a black blanket. My horse can't manage the stretch through the snow, and anyhow I can't leave the children alone, says the innkeeper, and so naturally we promise him to take his dead wife along with us the next morning, we, says Father, he says: Or rather: I promise him to get his dead wife into the next village for him, where they know the innkeeper and his wife, where they shall immediately relieve us of the wife if we but say her name. In gratitude the innkeeper falls to our feet, the coachman just grumbles and mumbles, and I have to promise him a little more money than we agree on before we depart from my village on the previous day so as to appease him so that he doesn't throw us, the innkeeper's dead wife and me, out of the sleigh. Chava Nechama is my wife's name, the innkeeper impresses upon me before we set off, she is the daughter of Raphael Michael, he says, so that I can hand her over properly in the next village, Without the name, he says, they don't take her from you, and so, nodding goodbye to the innkeeper and his waving children, I climb onto the box beside the coachman, murmuring Chava Nechama, daughter of Raphael Michael, so that I don't forget the name of the innkeeper's wife, Chava Nechama, daughter of Raphael Michael, I murmur to myself and against the coachman's resentful mumbling. So this is the burden that I take upon myself, that, though I only mean well, nearly brings me misfortune: The innkeeper and his children behind us before the house, the wife of the innkeeper, Chava Nechama, daughter of Raphael Michael, behind us on the sleigh, the coachman mumbling to himself, A white horse and a dead woman in the sleigh, and, Surely it can hardly get any worse, the snowstorm immediately, scarcely do we depart from the inn, breaking out over us, which my stubborn and silent coachman registers with nothing but a fierce, silently angry nod and with the words: So it can after all. We lose our way in the driving snow, scarcely do we depart from the inn and the poor innkeeper surrounded by his flock of children, continuing to wave for a long time before the inn in the middle of the South Lithuanian heath, which has been snow-covered for weeks. Chava Nechama, daughter of Raphael Michael, I murmur, Chava Nechama, daughter of Raphael Michael, now against the coachman's mumbling beside me and against the howling storm. On the black cover over the innkeeper's wife behind us, the snow, after a good hour, lies a hand's breadth high, the panic-stricken horse bites at the strap of its blanket and tries again and again to shake off the blanket, after two hours in the snowstorm we suspect that we're already so far off the correct course that it seems unimaginable how we're ever going to find our way out of the storm and back on course again. Chava Nechama, I murmur, and forget the name of her father, after four hours, against the wind and against the falling snow we can still see only as far as the horse's head and nothing beyond, but we may not stop. Chava, I murmur and forget her last name, remember her father's again at least, Raphael Michael, after eight hours in the snowstorm the horse bites through the strap of its blanket, the blanket vanishes behind us in the snowstorm, and after another two hours in the snowstorm we cross our own tracks for the first time. For a short time the name of the woman escapes me completely, after another four hours in the snowstorm and in a circle, in the gradually subsiding wind, we find the horse blanket directly beside the sleigh in the snow, we cross our own tracks for the second time, the father's name at least, Raphael Michael, returns, and after almost sixteen hours in the snowstorm and in a circle we take the blanket for the second time from the snow back into the sleigh, And the commandant actually asks me, says Marek: I can tell by looking at you, you want just as much as I do to go hunting now, he says: I like that, he says: You can have your week off so you can get married and do whatever else, he looks at me, and though only moments before I'm completely certain that the commandant tonight, on the night of his birthday, is drunk as I only rarely see someone drunk, his eyes are now completely sober, the commandant looks at me stone-cold sober, he turns away, he says: It doesn't quite want to get light today, does it, and leaves. He leaves. I suppose that I too may now go, I go, that's all. The commandant lets me go, I go, but in truth, says the Kradejew veterinarian sitting in Krystowczyk's kitchen, a glass of water in one hand, a cup of coffee in the other, incessantly blinking, in truth, says the Kradejew veterinarian, the commandant suddenly stops once again at the railing before you and stands there silently, doesn't he, in truth, says and lies the Kradejew veterinarian, he stands before you, doesn't leave, doesn't even think of leaving, instead remains silent for a few seconds, stands at the railing, remains silent, doesn't look at you, looks down into the woods, doesn't he, doesn't say a word for several minutes. In Krystowczyk's kitchen, the Kradejew veterinarian sits with a cup of coffee, with a glass of water and says to Marek and lies, while he looks alternately at Father, Wasznar, Antonina, never looks at Marek, once briefly looks at Krystowczyk, then briefly at Sapetow, but never at Marek: And then the commandant suddenly begins to speak, the Kradejew veterinarian says: He turns to you, doesn't he, and whispers: You can have your week off, and without comment pushes aside your right hand, which you, radiant with joy, immediately hold out to him, and pushes aside, without even taking notice of it, your left hand, which you, unfazed, relieved, hold out to him, and perhaps even shoves you away from him when you come toward him and, overjoyed, perhaps even want to hug him, he says: One condition, You say: Any condition, he says and stresses: One condition, he says to you: You can develop just as great a pleasure as mine in shooting and hunting. He says: And indeed can resolve not to shoot at buzzards as I do, but rather at pigs, if I so wish. From time to time perhaps also at sheep and goats, he says: For me. The Kradejew veterinarian says, lies, says Marek: And only now does he turn away, leave, and say softly to you as he goes: It doesn't quite want to get light today, does it, getting thicker and thicker the fog envelops the treehouse, and toward noon the little that we still see of what's taking place in our house and around our house hangs, swimming freely in the fog, before us, as if it's taking place neither here and now nor anywhere and anytime else. We sit in the treehouse and stare across to our house and to our garden, to the soldiers who sit in the garden behind the house, guard our house, and watch as their fellow soldiers completely refurnish our house, transform our house into a sort of administrative unit. We sit in the treehouse and stare across to the house in the fog and can't believe anything of the little that we discern, we sit stiffly and erectly and pressed as stiffly and erectly as possible against the treehouse walls, we stare through the hole that's supposed to be the frame for the treehouse door, the treehouse door is missing, the treehouse architect, Marek, says: As of June you two are aunts, and Zygmunt at five is already an uncle, Marek says: If you want to take her, if you want to hold her, he says: Go ahead and take her, and one evening in May it's pouring rain, it's one of the first long evenings of the year, Marek comes back from Jedenew in great haste in the car that he borrows from Father. He honks, he appears not even to have time before the departure from Jedenew to put the top up, honking he comes to a stop on the farm where we gather around the car, the interior of the car is ankle-deep under water, Marek doesn't stop honking, not even when he's long since stationary, he shouts, he drives the whole way here from Jedenew through the rain with the top open, he shouts: It's a girl, and one morning in May Marek climbs into the car that he buys in part with the money that he earns during the week for a few months as a sentry in the Nadice garrison and then on the weekend in Father and Wasznar's practice, that he buys in part with the money that Father and Wasznar lend him. In farewell he strokes our heads, gives us a poke in the upper arms and pushes us gently away from the car so he can open the driver's door and climb in and then pull the door shut behind him, he throws his suitcase behind him onto the backseat, and he looks at us for a long time, and he pulls Anna's clasp out of her hair, he takes the clasp out of her hand as Anna grasps at the clasp and tries to take the clasp back from him, he takes the clasp and lays it beside him on the passenger seat, he says: A remembrance. He leaves the engine running, he says to us: Look after Kacia and Zygmunt for me, and Father, and: And look after Wasznar for me, if you can, he says: I'm coming back the day after tomorrow. He says: I'm bringing Antonina along, and your little niece, he says: We're going to climb into the treehouse, all five of us, he says: Her name is Julia, and: The five of us, corrects himself and says: All six of us, he says: Her name is Julia, asks whether we don't also want to hold her, asks: Isn't she beautiful, and Marek says: As soon as we're back, we can finish building the treehouse, and he drives away, and he drives, and in the kitchen we already hear him honking, scarcely does he leave the place behind where the dirt road branches off toward us from the street that leads from Jedenew to Nadice, he turns off, and we hear him honking long before we see him racing at full speed along the dirt road toward our house and toward Wasznar and Antonina's farm behind our house and toward the old barn, the old barn between the two houses, which Wasznar years ago converts into a house for Antonina and Marek and Antonina and Marek's daughter, for a family. Behind the curtain on the kitchen window, behind the kitchen window, leaning on Kacia's counter, we think: It's only because of her that Marek comes racing through the pouring rain like mad, incessantly honking, toward our house, not because of us, and there, from the kitchen, we crouch beside each other on Kacia's counter, we look through the kitchen window across the fields and across the dirt road, we see Marek in his car leaving behind the turn-off of the dirt road into the street that connects Jedenew and Kradejew, driving toward Jedenew to pick up Antonina and the newborn girl, little Julia, our niece, from the Jedenew practice of the Jedenew doctor. In the kitchen, enveloped in the fragrance from Kacia's wonderful food, we think: Now he's picking them up from the Jedenew practice of the Jedenew doctor, his family, Antonina and little Julia, his family, we think: He promises nothing is going to change when he comes back, and so most surely everything is going to change when he comes back, or we think: He promises nothing is going to change when he comes back, and so most surely everything is going to remain as it is, or we think of nothing at all, don't know what we're thinking or are supposed to think, and thinking of nothing at all we stand beside each other leaning on Kacia's counter or slowly sit up straight beside each other against the inner wall of the treehouse, our stiff joints crack. We look across to our house and to our garden, we think: They're converting our house, everything's changing, nothing remaining. From the treehouse we look to the yard of our house and into the garden of our house and see Father's car in the distance standing unattended on the dirt road, and so we look carefully to the left, and so we look carefully to the right, before we, nearly every night by now, come at least once out of the field, grown more than head-high, onto the dirt road, see Father's car standing alone on the dirt road, whenever we go into the fields at night and come out of the fields at night to cross the dirt road, we look to the left and look to the right and see, either left or right of us depending where exactly we come out onto the dirt road from the field, Father's car standing on the dirt road. We try not to look at the car, not to see its dented hood when we, with an apron full of corncobs and sugar beets, cross the dirt road, as we agree neither of us two ever crosses the dirt road when she's out at night, and as we agree neither of us two ever looks, even only for a moment, over to Father's car standing unattended on the dirt road when we cross the dirt road indeed several times during the nights without admitting to even one of these crossings. Even on the third night Father's car is still standing unattended on the dirt road, traces of Marek and Krystowczyk are everywhere in the gravel on the dirt road and in the smashed-in hood, but neither Marek nor Krystowczyk is anywhere. We go one at a time. Each of us crosses the dirt road at least twice a night, while the other waits in the treehouse with growling stomach for what the other brings back from the fields, and each of us knows of the other, when she returns from the fields with a more or less filled apron, that the other, while she roams about in the fields for half the night, longer and longer from night to night, crosses the dirt road at least twice a night. We return from the fields to the woods and the treehouse in the middle of the night, take the block of wood out of its hiding place and whistle two brief thrush's whistles as Marek teaches us in weeks of work, when we return to the treehouse the other, even though we agree not to sleep while we're out in the fields at night, even though we agree to stay awake, to keep watch, is fully asleep and disheveled, and we sit down with our backs completely stiff against the wall as always or lie down on our bellies completely flat on the treehouse floor as always or lie down on our backs amid what we bring back from the fields, when the sky is clear and the stars are out, we lie down on our backs, clasp our hands under our heads, we do not breathe. We look at each other breathlessly, scarcely do we finally lie down, and we know, we think: She crosses the dirt road as I do before or as I too cross the dirt road when it's my turn to go next, we think: She doesn't have to admit it, we think: I know it, she knows it, it doesn't matter, nothing matters anymore, we think: It doesn't matter that we lie, deceive each other, downright shamelessly tell each other lies regularly by now, put something over on each other, we don't know what, nothing matters anymore. That, directly before our eyes, our house and all that we are is being emptied out. Lied to, deceived, bored, tired, disheveled, deceitful, lost, we think: No matter, and watch as all that we possess piles up ever higher, ever higher into a fire-heap, it's hard to believe how much we possess, we think: But that doesn't matter. It doesn't matter that two soldiers, before our eyes, are taking all that we possess and, depending on practical value, carrying it or throwing it out of the windows of our house into the garden, tables, chairs, two sinks, two portable washbasins, a washtub, linen armoires and cupboards, kitchen implements, filing cabinets, bookshelves and books, Father's secretaire, beds, carpets, lamps of all sorts, pillows and blankets, the stove, the kitchen table, a gramophone and record albums, Kacia's radio, the grand piano, curtains, the sofa and armchair, the sideboard, a coffee table, the serving cart, dressers, clothing, dolls, whole mountains of files, silverware by the box, glasses, cups, a typewriter, mirrors, a desk, two violin cases, notebooks, much more, carrying or throwing depending on practical value, without knowing what these things are for us. That down there two or three others then carry away from the window all of what we possess that they decide they can no longer use, pile it up somewhat farther back in the garden into a fire-heap to the left, into another heap to the right, we watch from the treehouse, at least they throw everything onto the fire-heap somewhat farther back in the garden to the left only after two or three of them in the garden determine at second or third glance before a record-keeper sitting in Father's rocking-chair that they indeed cannot or do not want to use the particular object, everything else goes onto the other heap in the back of the garden to the right. They pour gasoline over the heap to the left and then ignite it, stand for a long time beside one another around the fire and stand around uninvolved and with solemn faces, watch with interest those who take all of what we possess that they can still use, whole mountains of files, filing cabinets, the sideboard, silverware by the box, beds, bookshelves and books or notebooks, the grand piano, two violin cases, glasses, a gramophone and record albums, the stove, Kacia's radio, pillows and blankets, clothing, dressers, kitchen implements, the kitchen table, lamps of all sorts, dolls, a coffee table, a typewriter, a desk, the serving cart, the sofa, mirrors, two sinks, chairs, cups, carpets, tables and armchairs and Father's secretaire, curtains, cupboards, two portable washbasins, a washtub, linen armoires, load it all onto several trucks, and watch the fire as it burns up what they no longer let us be, but none of this matters anymore, we think: No matter. Marek says: Go ahead and take her, Julia, little Julia, he says, after we don't budge, after we stand still, put our hands silently in our pockets or clasp them behind our backs: Then you take the little one, Katarzyna, as he calls Katarzyna, Kacia, as we call her, whenever he wants to act highly formal, he says: Then you take the little one, Katarzyna, if you want, because he knows how happily Katarzyna, Kacia, would take Julia, if he'd only ask her. And so he gives her Julia, and so Kacia takes little Julia, our niece, our niece, our niece, Marek knows well or believes he knows well, even though we act defiant and act as if we don't want to take little Julia, that we'd like best to snatch little Julia from Kacia's arms so as to hold her at least just once very briefly and never again have to give her away, he knows it with certainty, we know it with certainty, but that doesn't matter. Two soldiers stop in a truck in front of the house and then wave two others away from the burning fire-heap and over to them. Together the four of them open the tarp over the tailgate at the rear of the truck and empty out the truck and then carry together what they take from the truck through the garden of our house and through the open kitchen door of our house into the house: typewriters, desks, filing cabinets, several reams of typewriter paper, bookshelves, chairs, armchairs, smoker's tables, cocktail tables, ashtrays, a bar. Meanwhile and afterward, in our garden behind our house a not precisely determinable number of figures stand motionlessly around the fire for hours and stare into the fire or stare at the incessant coming and going of other soldiers, countless other trucks, into our garden and out of our garden, ultimately, hours later, they turn away from the fire and turn away from the trucks incessantly driving to and fro, arriving, departing, loaded, not loaded, and vanish into the house or vanish into the street in front of the house or vanish somewhere in the fog, we persuade ourselves that they vanish because they themselves don't believe what they're doing, naturally we're mistaken. We persuade ourselves that we feel the heat of the fire coming up into the treehouse, sitting in the treehouse a good one hundred meters away from the fire in the garden we believe that we feel the heat of the fire even in the treehouse, we believe that because those are our things, our family's things that are burning there in the garden of our house, the fire, despite burning a good one hundred meters away from the treehouse and burning over there in the garden behind our house without regard to us, manages to singe our hair and to singe our eyebrows even here in the treehouse, naturally we're mistaken. We persuade ourselves, now that the baby's finally here, our niece, now that Antonina's back, and Marek finally no longer has to drive away, to drive every other day to Jedenew to the practice of the Jedenew doctor to see Antonina and the baby, that we finally have Marek back to ourselves. Everything's going back to the way it is all our life already, and we believe it's not going to be long now, it's May, until all five of us, six of us, counting little Julia now, our niece, go back outside together, climb back into the treehouse together to finish building the treehouse finally, as we agree with Marek, in spring, sitting on the window ledge or on the arm of the living room armchair, as Marek promises us, in spring.

Naturally we're mistaken, and Marek tells us: On the way from the garrison back along the country road toward Jedenew in the middle of the night, scarcely an hour after the commandant decides to make an exception and give me a week off for our wedding, I again and again fall asleep briefly in the car at the steering wheel, my chin on my chest albeit only for a few seconds each time, but again and again long enough to come dangerously near to the roadside, the ditch along the roadside. I nod off, murmur to myself in half-sleep, awake with a start, and then it's already almost morning when Anna finally returns from the fields to the treehouse. She apologizes, she recounts that when she's all of a sudden standing at the clearing in the field in the middle of the night, she can't help but lie down in the clearing as we lie this summer all summer long beside one another in the clearing nearly every single evening, she apologizes, she says: I can't help it, she explains: I stand at the edge of the clearing and contemplate the clearing for a long time and stand and think for a long time of the night two nights ago, the last of so many that we spend together in the clearing, and so I go into the clearing two nights after the two of us lie beside each other all night long for the hundredth time, for the last time this summer, in the circle of the clearing, without looking at each other, without speaking in the snowstorm threatening to smother us, ask: What now. You must imagine our situation, you must imagine how relieved we are when not only the wind gradually abates but also, very slowly, now the snowfall too, just imagine: We lose our way in a snowstorm, scarcely do we set off with the innkeeper's wife behind us on the sleigh, we lose our way, Father recounts, but the coachman sits beside me with the same immobile facial expression with which he picks me up in front of my parents' house the day before, with which he sits beside me since then without saying much. He merely stares ahead into the fog or into the wind, which is becoming more and more violent with the increasing duration of the trip and all of a sudden downright exploding, I struggle in vain now to discern anything at all. The coachman looks silently ahead, the wind whistles, and solely, says Father, by the fact that he wrinkles his forehead am I able to discern that the coachman even registers the storm, the snow, the wind, the cold. To discern something beyond that, to discern, for example, says Father, how he's doing, is impossible. He sits, huddles up to the side to avoid the wind, says

Father, an old man whose movements don't correspond to his age, who comes across as much younger than he evidently is, who obstinately speaks not one unnecessary word and drives the horse in front of his sleigh stubbornly through the snowstorm and in a direction that he can actually only suspect and hope is the right one. For hours we go around in circles, the wind gradually abates, the snowfall comes down less and less, and still there's not the least hint of where we're heading and where we actually must head, in which direction we must head and now in fact head can at the very most only be surmised. Perhaps we're long since heading back yet again, I say to the coachman, says Father, and lie, says Anna, during the night two nights ago in the circle of the clearing, the two of us, without speaking, or sit up only for a few moments and take turns standing up again and again to stretch. When we stand up to stretch, to move a little so that we don't freeze to death, we must take care that the horse doesn't lose the rhythm, we crouch back to back and lie on our backs and lie in the straw in the middle of the field on our bellies and lie on our sides, we stand up so as not to freeze to death, we swing our arms and stand up and sit down and stand again and, lying on the ground in the field, draw our knees to our chests and stand up carefully to look carefully across the grain to Wasznar and Antonina's farm, sit down again, make windmill-wheels with our arms in the ice-cold air, the innkeeper's wife under the cover behind us, funny, says Father, he says, he thinks: Funny, we are three, the coachman, the horse and I, but are actually four, the coachman, the horse, I and the dead woman behind us under the cover, and lie across each other like an X on our backs and lie like a T taking turns laying our heads on each other's bellies, we lie and crawl to the edge of the clearing so as to see something and crawl carefully a few meters into the grain so as to see something and test which of us two dares go farther into the grain, and play with Marek's long kitchen knife, his bread knife, and teach ourselves how to stab with it, and teach ourselves how to cut away with it the grain that stands in the way as we run by, and teach ourselves how to cut away with it the grain that stands in the way as we run by fleeing, but are by now perhaps long since heading in the right direction, says Father, where we are, says Father, he says, he can't yet even surmise in the middle of the snowstorm. Scarcely thirty minutes later we cross our own tracks in the snow for what is by now perhaps already the third or fourth time or teach ourselves how to hold each other as long and quietly as possible in a headlock, and lie down and breathe as quietly as possible and move forward as quietly as possible in the circle of the clearing, and jump up as quietly as possible and venture into the grain almost as far as the place on the dirt road where Marek lies, and try to move along in the grain as quietly as possible without losing our orientation. Into the collar of his jacket the coachman curses the horse, the winter, the weather, he curses, says Father, me and the innkeeper the most, and after each of his curses takes small sips from a bottle that he pulls out of his jacket, cursing me and the innkeeper most of all, and when he sees that I'm observing him through a hole in my blanket, he gestures to me to stand up and move so that I don't freeze to death, and so I stand up and, standing on the coach box, move my upper body back and forth and to and fro as carefully as possible and, standing on the coach box, go down slowly on my knees, straighten up again, take another sip from the bottle, sit down and try not to fall asleep, not to freeze to death, I have to hold the reins, the coachman too now moves beside me on the box so as not to freeze to death before we lie down and lie beside each other and take turns sleeping while the one on watch keeps watch, and beyond the field Wasznar and Antonina's farm burns. During our watch we jump up again and again as quietly as possible at even the slightest sound, and finally both fall asleep in spite of the bawling Jedenew farmers and then lie awake for the greater part of the night, holding each other's hands. Risk being smothered by the snow, but may not stop, lest the horse freeze to death, and so just lie and do not move, we cannot move, we do not breathe, we cannot breathe, we just lie and listen to the sounds that come from the dirt road very near to us and from our house, from the garden behind the house and from the pond. That come from Wasznar and Antonina's burning farm, and lie and do not look at each other, cannot look at each other, wonder again and again what we're doing here, how we come to be here, and lie and see nothing more, cannot look at each other, and perceive from out of night and fog nothing more than sounds. Many hours later, says Father, only when we're already sure that it's all over, the snow then completely stops falling, the wind abates, and frozen half-to-death, smothered half-to-death, says Father, starved half-to-death, the horse half-dead, says Father, we stand before a pond, the pond behind the house. Directly before us, says Father and grins, before us lie Wasznar's farm and our house in the middle of the snow, the coachman and I think of and believe in a village, perhaps even the village to which we're supposed to bring the innkeeper's wife, I ask the coachman if he still knows her name, but the coachman doesn't answer, he jumps down from the box and walks toward the house behind the pond. He laughs, we don't believe a word he says. There's almost nothing we'd rather do than listen to his stories, especially this one story. And this is true even though the story that he tells us, this exact one, which he tells us for years already when he wants to tell us or has to tell us because we want him to and ask him, downright force him, again and again, again and again, innumerable times, at all possible opportunities over the years, to tell us how he, and so we too, come to be here on our farms close to Jedenew, this very story we already discover years ago in a book in his library. Since then, even still today, we again and again read the story from the book to each other, even though we already know for a long time that Father tells us this story that's not his so often already as his own. That doesn't bother us. For everything that happens at our home close to Jedenew is a story, we determine and decide, when we consult about how we're going to deal from now on with the fact that Father's story is not his at all, that he only pilfers his story from here and there and devises it as his, that we know nothing about his true story, and so also don't know how he actually in reality comes to be on the farms close to Jedenew, but we decide that this story that he pilfers from here and there and devises as his is now, for us, his story, just as everything else around us is only a story that can just as well be an invention as Father's. That we preserve and keep for ourselves, or forget, or someday pass on, or can only remember for ourselves, once, twice, more often, and then can forget when we want, or must forget when nothing else is possible. But always remember and must remember again one last time when, as we decide, we have no other choice. In the treehouse with our backs against the treehouse walls, we remember that Father repeats, Before us our house, that he adds: The house that is ours today. The coachman and his white horse, the snowstorm and the innkeeper's dead wife, says Father, ultimately bring me nothing but good fortune.

Anna says she falls asleep in the clearing, scarcely does she lie down. The vegetables that she gathers in the fields lie scattered around her in the clearing, it's already almost morning, already almost daylight, when Anna finally returns to the treehouse. She apologizes, she says she passes by the clearing only by chance on her way through the fields, and once again she can't help but stop in the clearing, she says, she simply can't help but lie down in the clearing, lie down on her back in the straw, she says, she's sorry that she lies down in the clearing yet again contrary to our agreement, at the same moment that she lies down in the clearing she's already sorry, she says: Even though it's so wonderful to lie there as before, and from this night on each of us, contrary to our agreement, lies at least once a night in the clearing when we take turns going out into the fields to fetch what we need. We take turns leaving the treehouse, first one of us goes, then the other goes, if the one goes first, then the other goes roughly three hours after the first returns, and because she can't wait any longer to get to the clearing and into the clearing, after a few nights the first scarcely sits in the treehouse again when she already sets off, from night to night we go earlier into the fields from the treehouse, from night to night we stay away longer and come back to the treehouse from night to night later and later, so as to be able to stay away and lie in the clearing as long as possible, then after a few nights it's scarcely dark when the first already runs over the ridge under cover of the trees, under cover of the grain we go each night a different, less and less haphazard, more and more direct way through the fields and across the dirt road to the clearing, through the last meters of grain we go as carefully as possible in fear of coming upon one of the Jedenew farmers or the Kradejew veterinarian in the clearing. At times we downright expect to come upon one of the Jedenew farmers or the Kradejew veterinarian sometime awaiting us in the clearing, our hearts skip a beat as we carefully bend apart the last rows of grain to cast a first glance at the clearing in the night, in our excitement along the whole way from the treehouse to the clearing we can scarcely breathe for fear, we go nonetheless. We set off, from night to night we leave the treehouse earlier and go the way from the treehouse to the clearing from night to night more and more quickly, and from night to night go a less and less careful way to the clearing, and though we must sometimes search awhile until we find the clearing, we always find the clearing, naturally it's Marek who's the first to find the exact place where we already, last year as well as all the years before that we can remember, cut a clearing in the grain. Marek stops, the scythe in his hands and his bare legs cut up, scratched up by the wheat, he bends down to tie his laces, he stands up and he says: Here it is, and begins cutting the clearing in the field. Marek says the place where he cuts the clearing in the field every year for years already, where Father too cuts the clearing in the grain virtually every year prior to that, is the best place to cut a clearing in the field, without ever exactly revealing to us why. It just is. It is as Marek says, we need no explanation, everything is as he says, as always, we nod in agreement, as always, as always without knowing why. Anna cries: That's right, and lets herself fall backwards laughing into the grain, there where we're going to cut the clearing in the grain as we do every year, lying on the ground she cries: So let's get started. And so Antonina comes onto the wooden dock to press crushed ice wrapped in a towel as carefully as possible on Marek's split-open, sutured, swollen eyebrow. Marek resigns himself to it, the scythe leans against the back of the house. With one hand Marek holds sleeping Julia, scarcely three weeks old, in his arm, our niece, our niece, with the other hand he strokes Zygmunt's head, he tells us: Only last week Father and I drive out to Krystowczyk's farm to slaughter twenty-five pigs dying of pig plague, already half-dead, on Krystowczyk's farm, and during the slaughter Krystowczyk sings softly in Russian, no doubt to mock us, Father and me. Marek says: Then very early this morning, only a few hours after the news of the dissolution of the Nadice garrison reaches Jedenew, scarcely two hours after the news of the dissolution of all hitherto existing garrisons this side of Bisa reaches Jedenew, on my way back to Jedenew along the Nadice country road from the garrison being dissolved in Nadice, Krystowczyk already sits in Jedenew alone on a bench under a tree in the Jedenew marketplace. I stop, climb out of the car, approach, give as friendly a greeting as possible in spite of the incident in Krystowczyk's kitchen last week, in spite of everything, and sit down beside him on the empty seat on the bench, I ask him about this and that, but Krystowczyk is heavily drunk, he doesn't reply. Only last week, late in the evening one evening, after Father and Marek and Wasznar and Antonina return from Krystowczyk's farm, while they recount what happens there in Krystowczyk's kitchen, we're suddenly so tired that we sit down beside one another in a circle and lie down on the wooden dock in the warm night and can hardly listen any longer to what happens in the evening in Krystowczyk's kitchen, and are hardly in a condition any longer to discuss what is to happen now. Wasznar sits on the bench against the back of the house. From in the water, Marek rests his elbows on the small wooden dock so as to listen to what he already knows, we others sit and crouch and lie dead tired around Father on the small wooden dock. Father holds on his knees the book from which he likes best to read, and takes the book from his knees, lays it carefully on the wooden dock beside him, tells us: And so Marek and I drive out today in the late afternoon to Krystowczyk's farm to slaughter twenty-five of Krystowczyk's pigs dying of pig plague. We arrive, we lead the pigs out of the sty, those pigs that we mark and isolate in a separate pen yesterday evening, and so Marek and I lead the pigs out of their separate pen in the sty one after another onto the meadow, and drive the pigs one after another across the meadow toward the slaughterhouse and there into a large enclosure. Twenty-five pigs, he says: Scarcely does an hour go by when Marek passes the captive-bolt gun from one hand into the other, wipes his wrists and forehead with a handkerchief, says: Done, takes a deep breath and looks at Krystowczyk, who stops singing, during the slaughter Krystowczyk sings softly in Russian. On the wooden dock, his feet in the water, Father says: I look at Marek standing beside me, he wipes the sweat from his forehead and finishes the work. He winds the cord of the captive-bolt gun and wipes the captive-bolt gun meticulously with a moist cloth, just as Wasznar and I teach him, and wraps it in a cloth, wraps tape meticulously around it, wipes the end of the cord meticulously and places both, gun and cord, back into the toolbox. He packs everything up meticulously and wipes his forehead again and again with his handkerchief, and scarcely forty minutes later we, Marek and I, still remain, after Krystowczyk is already long since in the house, in front of Krystowczyk's house for another moment, and stand before the horizon contracted into a strip, look at each other or look nowhere, and not until a good quarter of an hour after Krystowczyk do we slowly enter the house. Father leans back on the wooden dock with his arms stretched back, resting his weight on his hands on the wooden dock, he says: We sit in Krystowczyk's kitchen, as we do for years, for decades, whenever I work on his farm, as we go into Krystowczyk's kitchen for decades after my work on Krystowczyk's farm, to sit together some more, to make fried eggs and have something to drink, to talk, we sit, Krystowczyk, unhurriedly and without letting himself be distracted, fries eggs, as he always does. We, Marek and I, sit smoking silently at the kitchen table behind him, have something to drink, Marek spills some of his schnapps or beer, whatever, and Krystowczyk lets the eggs fry, wipes the pool rapidly spreading around our glasses on the checkered tablecloth into a small puddle, unhurriedly lets the puddle between our glasses soak into the tablecloth, after a while I say: You know I'm not interested in the money that I lend you for the farm, Krystowczyk, I say, says Father: I merely want to inquire how you're doing, I say: For four months I get no installments from you, and: Not that it matters to me or I even miss the money, by no means, I say: And not that I insist that you pay right on time every month, I say, and: You know that, and: But I nonetheless want to inquire how you're doing, whether there are problems, are you unable to pay, do you not have any money, I ask, Father tells us. I'm in no great hurry, he says, nervously taking a sip, he says to Krystowczyk's back: You know that. Do you need money, are you not doing well, he asks, and Krystowczyk turns around to the eggs, fries, says: You two slaughter an astonishing number of our pigs for the Russians lately, peppers, salts, crushes some garlic, I say: Don't worry, you don't have to pay everything if you can't, I say: I tell you from the beginning that I don't need the money, you know that you don't have to pay when you don't have it. We eat, we drink, Krystowczyk murmurs: An astonishing number of pigs and louder: Do you miss the money, do you need it urgently, even though he knows that I don't miss the money, that I don't miss it at all, and that I most surely don't need the money urgently, he says: Are you in a hurry, even though he knows full well that I'm anything but in a hurry, and so I say, says Father: Of course not, I'm not interested in the money, and Krystowczyk, more brusquely: Are you in a hurry, don't you trust me. I don't know what to say, as you can imagine, I say nothing for a while, Krystowczyk fries and repeats, somewhat more softly: Are you in a hurry, don't you trust me. He says: Don't worry, you're going to get your money by next month. I nod, says Father, I nod and say something like Good, all right, very good, I'm pleased, I'm glad to get away from the subject, and look over to Marek, who changes his seat, sits down opposite the puddle, Krystowczyk says: Lately you slaughter an astonishing number of pigs for the Russians, eating, drinking, we reply: The pig plague, Krystowczyk, and: Not for the Russians, Krystowczyk, and: For you, and Krystowczyk says: Ah, so it's the pig plague. We eat, we drink, we say: The pig plague, we say: They're helping you and the others by picking up the animals for you, incinerating them for you, and Krystowczyk fries the eggs, fries and says: Ah, the pig plague. He doesn't look up anymore from his fried eggs while we speak, explain ourselves, and Krystowczyk is still frying when, shortly thereafter, Sapetow's car stops in front of the kitchen window, he looks up only briefly from the fried eggs as his front door opens, he doesn't look as Sapetow stands in the doorway, the Kradejew veterinarian right behind him. Krystowczyk takes the eggs from the pan and serves them onto plates, pushes a plate to me, one to Marek, the third plate to Sapetow, who nods wordlessly and takes a seat in the armchair. He looks at the Kradejew veterinarian, the veterinarian, thanking him, shakes his head, the Kradejew veterinarian, says Sapetow, rarely has much more than water or coffee, the Kradejew veterinarian says: A glass of water would perfectly suffice, or a cup of coffee, and Krystowczyk unhurriedly refills our glasses, wipes up the last remains of the spilled drink from the tablecloth. He gestures to Sapetow to move from the armchair to Marek's old seat, and gives the Kradejew veterinarian a glass of water, a cup of coffee, Sapetow clears his throat. Starts to eat, the veterinarian sits down, drinks some water, ignores the coffee, drinks some water, pours milk in the coffee, clears his throat, drinks some coffee, Krystowczyk says softly: Ah, so it's the pig plague, and Marek and I eat more slowly, we do not breathe. We sit on this evening, on the last evening, in the garden of our house, Wasznar on the bench against the back of our house, we on the narrow wooden dock around father, we, that is, Katarzyna is there, Kacia, she sits somewhat apart on the ground in the grass. She sits there, draws up her knees under her chin, crosses her ankles and embraces her legs with her arms, Marek is there, he's the only one still in the water, resting his elbows on the end of the wooden dock from in the water, and Anna is there, still in her bathing suit, which she wears already all summer long because the bathing suits are Marek's birthday present to us, there's nothing both of us would rather wear this summer and we hardly ever wear anything other than these very bathing suits, and Anna, who hates nothing more than being disappointed, especially in summer, nothing more than that, as she says, she says: Nothing more, except perhaps to have to journey through a snowstorm for days and days with a corpse in the wagon and a coachman who speaks not a single word, to have to deliver the corpse with which I have not the slightest to do, without knowing exactly where in the middle of this deeply snow-covered South Lithuanian heath in deepest winter I lose my way, and actually to have other, more important things to do, she says and laughs. Julia is there, she lies in Antonina's arms, little Julia, and screams from time to time, during the greater part of the last four weeks she's asleep, and Zygmunt is there, who doesn't yet quite listen to what father is recounting, he sits on the wooden dock between us and tries to touch the water's surface with his hands from the wooden dock, and tries to scrape Marek's cigarette stubs and little pebbles out of the gaps between the planks of the wooden dock, he contemplates everything that he finds, collects it in his pants pockets or throws it into the pond, laughs and claps with glee over the little circles that the cigarette stubs, pebbles, sun-dried flower heads that he finds make in the water. And Antonina is there, Antonina sits, says Father, with Julia in her arms, between us on a kitchen chair at Krystowczyk's kitchen table, after she comes later together with Wasznar in the car to check on us and make sure everything's all right with us, to see where we are. On this evening several evenings later, on the last evening, Antonina sits with us on the wooden dock and again and again looks at Marek calmly and fixedly and proudly and closely for several minutes, and when she doesn't look at Marek, looks nowhere, into the water perhaps, at sleeping little Julia as she sleeps, into the fields, to the dirt road, to the ridge on the horizon, into the sky, and ultimately it is Antonina who one evening, on the last evening, is the first to see the Jedenew farmers. She listens to Father, who recounts what happens in Krystowczyk's kitchen, or listens to Marek's story about shooting buzzards for well over the hundredth time already, or listens to Marek's story about Krystowczyk in the Jedenew marketplace, as she sits and stares for a few seconds toward the gathering Jedenew farmers. Father says: Krystowczyk says: Ah, so it's the pig plague, and we eat more slowly, and ultimately it is Antonina who says softly: They're coming. When we jump up, run away, our punch glasses fall into the water or shatter on the wooden dock or spill out over Father's books, some of the books fall into the water as we run away, we do not breathe, softly, very softly, Krystowczyk sings songs in Russian during the slaughter, no doubt to mock us, Marek and me, says Father, and Marek lies beside us in the field and smiles as he sleeps, pretends he's asleep, he sits up and adjusts the pillow under his back, lets us crawl into his bed when we can't sleep, he sits up, rubs his hands together over the fire in the fireplace and takes a gingerbread out of the box sitting between him and Anna, in our pensive silence between two poems he puts Zygmunt in a headlock for fun or frolics with him across the meadow. Krystowczyk stands and fries and occasionally wipes the tablecloth, and wrinkles his forehead and hears the door opening as Wasznar and Antonina enter, sit down, but Krystowczyk doesn't look at them, says Father, doesn't look up from the brewing coffee that he freshly grinds beforehand, says Father, fresh beans, he says, we wonder where Krystowczyk gets fresh coffee beans as the Kradejew veterinarian clears his throat, looks at his pocket watch and clears his throat once again, stands up briefly, smoothes his pants, coughs, looks at his pocket watch, takes a sip of water and nods with thanks for a schnapps set down before him, takes a sip of coffee, clears his throat, says: Now then, and: What do you still want, go away, murmurs Krystowczyk on the bench in the Jedenew marketplace, And what I want, says Marek, I myself don't quite know. Perhaps I simply want to sit there, to remain sitting in peace, the Nadice garrison is officially being dissolved this morning, I have off, I don't yet know what's happening, so I simply don't reply and, rather taken aback, pick up from the ground an envelope that Krystowczyk, with the words I'm on my way to your place, throws at my feet. Krystowczyk murmurs: The last installment, and I open the envelope, but instead of the balance of the amount that Father lends him many years ago, some time, says Father, after I arrive many years ago together with Krystowczyk here on the farms close to Jedenew, that Father lends him, says Marek, so that Krystowczyk can buy his own farm, there is only a single small bill, much less than what's still outstanding, as I happen to know, but Krystowczyk says: That's the last installment, now we're even. I don't know what to say, says Marek, I want to be very careful and explain that he knows well that he doesn't have to give Father the whole installment, and especially not more or even the whole outstanding amount, if he can't. He knows that he can pay and also only has to pay as much as he's able to pay when he's in a position to pay, I assert as carefully as possible that in fact somewhat more than what is in the envelope is still outstanding, that this, however, by no means matters to Father, for if Krystowczyk can't pay, then he doesn't have to pay, then he doesn't pay for just as long as he can't pay, he knows that, I say. I say that Father by no means needs the money, that Krystowczyk can go ahead and take his time with the installments, if there's no other way, I say everything that Father already tells him a good week earlier in his kitchen, but Krystowczyk doesn't listen to me. He says: The last installment, and turns away, and so I simply sit for quite a while beside Krystowczyk on the bench in the morning sun, listen to his drunken murmuring and muttering, and again and again almost have to smile a little while I sit beside him, because in spite of everything and even though I'm taking pains to be very careful, it's hard to take Krystowczyk seriously as drunk as he is, because Krystowczyk, so drunk here on the bench in the Jedenew marketplace, behaves almost like a defiant little kid, almost a little like you from time to time, Anna, Marek says with a laugh. Kacia comes from the house with a tray of apple pie or Father comes, also from the house, with a glass of the first and last summer punch of the year for each of us, Marek tells us: And so we sit awhile on the bench under the tree in the sun without speaking, nearly a whole hour goes by without my noticing. We sit, the garrison in Nadice is being dissolved, and not until much later, hours later, indeed perhaps not even until now do I understand that that hour together with Krystowczyk in the Jedenew marketplace this morning is the only hour in a very, very long time during which neither of us two, neither Krystowczyk nor I, precisely knows what's going to happen in Jedenew and close to Jedenew and anywhere else at all. The garrison is withdrawing, and no one is there yet to take its place, and so for a few moments there is not really anything for either of us two to do or to say, we can only suspect what's coming, and both suspect the same thing, but we don't yet know anything, and so we just sit, we do not speak and scarcely move, there is nothing to say and there is nothing to do. The sun rises higher, it's silent, it's getting warmer, and I enjoy this one hour in utter silence beside Krystowczyk during which I don't have to think much because nothing is happening. Until it's ultimately time to go. When I stand up, say goodbye and go back to the car, Krystowczyk also jumps up and pushes me in the back. I fall and he jumps onto me as I'm lying on the ground so that he can pin me to the ground with his knees on my chest and spit in my face and can scream, Don't worry, I'm going to pay, and, Ah, so it's the pig plague, and punch me in the face, and can scream, Don't worry, you're going to get your money and, Ah, so it's the pig plague and goat plague and sheep plague, yanks my hair, throws sand from the ground in my face, throws a handful of sand and small stones in my face, spits in my face and stands up again and walks away, and as he walks away, suddenly sober, wide-awake and a little frightened by what he says and does, casts a frightened and furtive glance back at me, still in uniform, albeit a dusty, torn uniform, my army cap battered in the dirt. I remain lying, I'm bleeding in the face, I don't know exactly where. I remain lying, I lie in the middle of the field as always in the clearing, and scarcely do I lie down when I immediately fall asleep, as always, says Anna, she says she doesn't wake up until she hears voices nearby. She says she looks around. Krystowczyk's voice is among the voices, she says, she stands up, looks anxiously around, for Krystowczyk knows that we're still here somewhere in the area. He sees us coming out of the field together with Marek and Zygmunt onto the dirt road, together with Zygmunt following Marek out of the field onto the open dirt road and walking across the dirt road, a good stretch along the dirt road toward Father's car, which is still parked unattended on the dirt road, toward him, Krystowczyk, he knows that we're missing, she says: Sapetow too sees us, Sapetow and Krystowczyk know that we're still here somewhere in the area, they know we're nearby, and: Soon they're going to search for us, and know we're not very far, we can't be far, they shouldn't even have to search for us within all too large a radius and says: We can consider ourselves lucky if Krystowczyk doesn't remember the treehouse. If Krystowczyk doesn't assume what he should in fact assume, he knows us, after all, long and well enough: Namely, says Anna, that we don't leave. Anna is the first to dare, on our third day in the treehouse, to let her legs dangle out of the treehouse into the open in broad daylight, Anna says: Two pirates. She says: The two of us.

Marek takes the crushed ice wrapped in a towel away from his temple, but Antonina immediately guides his hand back again, Marek tells us: And so I come home from Nadice beaten positively black and blue. It's summer, it's June or July or August, we sit together and Marek tells his story or we read from books together, we read or get read to when we're too tired to keep reading ourselves, Father reads, and in winter he calls up to us in our rooms, he calls us down from our rooms into the living room to read with him, in winter he says: Katarzyna, as he calls Kacia whenever he wants to be solemn, he says: Katarzyna, Kacia, as we on the other hand call her, is making you hot milk, then in summer, in June, July, August, he says solemnly: Katarzyna is making you lemonade with crushed ice, he says in winter very solemnly: Katarzyna is also serving you cookies and cake, in summer he says: Some fresh fruit, if you want, or compote, if you'd like, in winter he says: Katarzyna, please make me tea, or: Katarzyna, if you could please pour me a cognac, in winter he calls us down into the living room, downstairs in the living room he says: Sit down, he says: We're reading fairy tales, legends, poems together, poems from Germany, in summer, only three days ago or four, in June, he spends the whole warm afternoon in the kitchen by the radio and after the latest news about the invasion calls us away from our work on the treehouse, out of the woods and to the pond in the garden behind the house, he says: Sit down, we sit on the floor gathered around the fireplace and sit beside one another in the garden on the garden bench that we paint ourselves last summer, blue, green, red, sit around a large garden table and sit in the evening behind the house in the midsummer sun on the narrow wooden dock that leads out into the pond behind the house, and sit and lie and swim in the sun and sit together reading and drink the first and last summer punch of the year, swim and splash one another with water, for the last time. We sit, nine in number as we are this year, or eight in number as last summer, or seven in number in the previous years, we listen to Father who reads from his books, we count the mosquito bites on our legs and braid each other's hair. We lie in the grass behind the house stretched out in the sun, we take Zygmunt by his arms and legs and, laughing, throw him as far into the pond as we can, we drink summer punch, each of us a glassful, when we sit outside on the wooden dock in the garden behind the house, and one evening, on the last

evening, on the wooden dock behind the house Antonina
suddenly says softly: They're coming. We sit wrapped in
blankets beside one another on the sofas and close
together around the fireplace in the living room and sit,
in the bathing suits that Marek gives us for our birthday,
by the pond or in the grass in the garden, we see, across
the golden fields and in the distance, a deer leaping out
of the woods into a field lying fallow this summer, and in
winter Kacia serves us hot milk and hot malt coffee on a
tray on the living room table and in summer serves us a
large pitcher of lemonade with crushed ice swimming in
the lemonade on a tray on the garden table and in winter
Kacia brings Father his tea, his cognac on a tray in the
living room and serves us cookies that we bake together
with her in winter, in December, because it's customary,
as she says, as she says again and again each winter, each
December and each year in the pre-Christmas period,
because it's what's done, as she says, she says: It's simply
what's done, she says: In the pre-Christmas period one
simply bakes spritz cookies, and she bakes spritz cookies.
She says: In the pre-Christmas period one simply bakes
fruit bread, and she bakes fruit bread, several canisters.
She says: One bakes Berlin bread, and she bakes Berlin
bread by the box, she says: Shortbreads, and bakes
shortbreads, a whole cupboard full, and she says:
Gingerbreads, and she bakes dozens of boxes of
gingerbreads on baking wafers and gingerbreads coated
with chocolate on both sides and lets the gingerbreads
cool overnight in the pantry while she bakes spritz
cookies, we help her. We get to paint the gingerbreads
with food coloring after Kacia must more or less force us

to after we're very uncertain before Father about what we may and may not do in the pre-Christmas period and after Kacia must badger Father for several days so that he allows us to paint the gingerbreads that she bakes each year as she does every year, visibly annoyed he says to us: Do whatever you want, as always, and so he lets us paint the gingerbreads, pipe multicolored icing from a pastry bag onto the gingerbreads, and so he lets us spend every afternoon for whole weeks of the pre-Christmas period together with Kacia in the kitchen while it snows, lets us bake together with Kacia without trying to keep us away from Kacia and Kacia's Christmas baking as he tries to do every year until now at least for a few weeks before he, every year, at some point gives up with a sigh. And so, as he does every year, he ultimately, albeit reluctantly, lets us bake Christmas cookies together with Kacia after all, while we squirt food coloring and Kacia is busy at the oven with the baking sheets and her thick baking mitts Kacia says softly to us: It's Chanukah, but you may not celebrate Chanukah, because your father doesn't want you to celebrate Chanukah. She says: And it's Christmas, but you may not celebrate Christmas because your father by no means wants you to celebrate Christmas, she says: But you have to celebrate something. We sit, take the gingerbreads from her off the baking sheet, stuff the still hot, soft gingerbreads into our mouths with both hands and take the icing from her and, kneeling, nodding, wide-eyed, paint the gingerbreads, we chew, we say: You're right, and that she is. Kacia serves us a large dish with cut-up fruit, small slices of apples, pears, plums, cherries, and seven small dishes with sweet, sticky, wonderfully cinnamony apple compote, and so we sit and drink hot milk or malt coffee in winter because we're freezing, and drink lemonade in summer to combat the heat, and watch Father drinking his tea, his cognac, staring away for a long time into emptiness, into darkness, into the fireplace, into the lake, into the sun, into the fields, for several minutes he stares, silently sipping at his tea, at his cognac in Mother's wing chair or deck chair before he reaches for his books. We sit in a circle around the fireplace. We sit cross-legged in bathing suits on the small wooden dock or let our legs dangle in the water. Lie on our backs or on our bellies, swim, dive, jump and must take care as we do that Father's books, which we stack beside us on the wooden dock, don't get wet, for the first time ever in all the years that we sit together in summer on the narrow wooden dock that, behind the house, leads out into the pond behind the house, and read, get read to, read to one another, in spite of Father's admonitions to be careful, some of his books get wet when Antonina one evening, on the last evening, looks toward the dirt road and says softly: They're coming. When we jump up, run away, our punch glasses fall into the water or shatter on the wooden dock or spill out over Father's books, some of the books fall into the water as we run away. We sit down, we sit and we observe the snow outside the window or observe the snow on the windowsill, we observe the snow that breaks away from the chimney ledge and falls down into the fireplace and immediately dissolves into a cloud of steam. We sit wrapped in blankets around the fireplace or close together on the sofa and draw pictures and drink and read, Father reads, he reads and we sit and crouch and lie in the clearing in the grain field, Marek tells his story. He holds in his hand a chewed chicken bone that he gnaws at for several moments as if the bone could actually still yield something, he says: So that's what happens with shooting buzzards, my story, an amusing story, we sit and crouch and lie on the wooden dock, Marek tells his story and holds in his hand an apple and some crushed ice wrapped in a towel, he says: And so that's what happens with Krystowczyk, he says sadly: Also an amusing story, isn't it, and takes the chicken bone out of his mouth and throws the chicken bone behind him into the field and takes the apple core out of his mouth and throws the apple core from the small wooden dock over the pond and over the garden and over the meadow behind the house into the field. We sit and we lie and we no longer talk much, soon we fall asleep, one after another, with heavy eyes, without fighting any longer against sleep, without even wanting to fight any longer against sleep, with a warm feeling everywhere in our bodies. Anna lays her head carefully on Antonina's belly, which is already as big as a pumpkin, and Zygmunt's head lies on Antonina's belly, Marek lies stretched out long on his back in the clearing in the field, and Antonina lays her head on his belly while his fingers twitch as if he were softly playing piano while he's asleep, and his eyelids twitch as if he weren't asleep at all while he's asleep, as if he were awake, though he's asleep, and as if he were lying awake while only pretending to be asleep as we others too are asleep.

Shortly before she falls asleep, Antonina lays her hand on Anna's and Zygmunt's heads on her belly, Antonina says to Anna and Zygmunt on her belly: Listen closely, listen to her moving. She's moving toward us, listen to her, and so Father then begins, as loudly as he can, to read against our frolicking and jumping and splashing in the pond behind the house. He reads loudly: For a thousand years already and longer, we sit close beside each other or Anna sits alone exhausted, breathless and with her eyes opened wide to the stars, with her back leaning against the treehouse wall, as always, or lies breathlessly as always, completely flat on her belly on the treehouse floor or on her back on the treehouse floor, above her the black treetops, the sky. She gasps for air, a good half a meter of rope-ladder dangles down from the treehouse into the faraway open, so that the rope-ladder doesn't betray us we together pull it up into the treehouse as quietly as possible and together lay the rope-ladder on the treehouse floor as quietly as possible, as always. So that she doesn't betray us, we together press our hands over Anna's mouth, over Anna's rattling breath, Anna gasps out: I simply can't help but go into the clearing, she says: I simply can't help it, she says: I must do it. She says she can't help it, she does it. She lies down, she falls asleep, scarcely does she lie down there in the clearing where we lie four nights ago probably for the hundredth time already, for the last time. Lie beside each other for a whole last night in the circle of the clearing, lie without looking at each other and ask without speaking: What now, and lie in the circle of the clearing, the two of us, and lie in the circle of the clearing without speaking, sit and stand up only for a few moments to stretch and crouch back to back and stand up carefully and look carefully across the grain and see Wasznar and Antonina's farm burning, crawl to the edge of the clearing so as to see something and crawl carefully a few meters into the grain so as to see something and test who dares go farther into the grain, and play with Marek's long kitchen knife, his bread knife, and teach ourselves how to stab with it, and lie down, breathe as quietly as possible, and move as quietly as possible in the circle of the clearing and jump up as quietly as possible and venture into the grain almost as far as the place on the dirt road where Marek lies, and try to move along in the grain as quietly as possible without losing our orientation, and lie down, lie beside each other and take turns sleeping while the other keeps watch, and jump up again and again during our watch as quietly as possible at even the slightest sound nearby, and finally both fall asleep for only a moment, then lie awake for the greater part of the night, holding each other's hands, directly before our pond behind the house we stop. The coachman clicks his tongue, the horse stops, exhausted to death. A short distance away on the side of the house facing the yard and behind the poplars the gable of Wasznar's farm shines against the blue sky opening up behind Wasznar's farm. The wind coming from the fields shakes the snow in great clouds from the poplars, under the poplars stands a snowman, and in the house directly before us sit seven or eight people behind thickly steamed-up windows at breakfast or lunch or afternoon coffee. I don't know how long we're underway in the snowstorm, says Father, a day and a night perhaps, perhaps longer. When we arrive, it's impossible to judge what time it is, Perhaps morning, says the coachman, panting from his seat on the bench behind the house, on which Wasznar always sits these days, which you paint last summer, says Father, when he tells the story, his story, after we paint the bench, or says: That you should paint sometime, if you have the time and desire to do so this summer, the lacquer is already old, since back then, he says, since the day we arrive here close to Jedenew, the bench looks like it does today, never different, always with the same lacquer, never different, he says, when he tells the story before we paint it, blue, green, red, Perhaps noon or afternoon, says the coachman, catching his breath, from the bench, and beats the snow from his clothes. Back then we sit for a long time on the bench behind the house, without the people in the house, in the house that is ours today, even noticing us. We still believe that with this first house behind the pond, which is our house today, a village begins, perhaps even the village we're looking for, and so I try desperately to remember the name of the innkeeper's wife, I remember Chava, nothing else, and somewhat at a loss I give, we give, says father, the horse a drink from a cracked open trough in the yard, we give the horse some hay from a winter store in Wasznar's stable, without anyone noticing us, we sit on the bench and watch the clouds opening up more and more, Perhaps already nearly evening, says the coachman and rolls himself a cigarette, the first since we leave the inn. Your mother, says Father, back then the same age as you are now, Father always says, no matter when he tells us the story, is the first to discover us, the coachman, the horse and the sleigh, the dead woman and me, back then I'm the same age as Marek today. She's the first who discovers us sitting on the bench behind the house when she decides to open the window for a moment from the dining table, below her on the bench sit the coachman and I beside each other, still covered with snow from head to foot, with red faces and beards full of snow and ice, glad that we're alive, that the horse is alive, we take a breather and don't talk to each other, after a while and not until long after your mother calms down from her fright in the face of the two strangers on the bench behind her house, and Wasznar, Antonina's mother and your grandfathers and grandmothers carefully lower and lay aside the shotguns, spades, hayforks and dungforks they're pointing at us, even though the name of the woman on the sleigh simply refuses to come to my mind, the only thing that I believe, while Wasznar, Antonina's mother and your grandfathers and grandmothers stand before us thus armed, can save us from the shotguns, spades, hayforks and dungforks, only the name, because I'm convinced that either Wasznar or Antonina's mother or your grandfathers and grandmothers would know and recognize it if only it would come to my mind, the coachman, cheerful and still sitting with me on the bench behind the house smoking one cigarette after another, even though the people in the house, for whatever reason, when I ask them about it later they give no reply, long since invite and ask us to come into the house, have something to eat, warm up, change our clothes, introduces himself to me. He says, says Father, his name is Krystowczyk, we don't believe a word he says. I too introduce myself, says Father, and it is the coachman, supposedly Krystowczyk, as Father claims, Krystowczyk, the coachman, who, still on the same day, behind our house in the garden on the garden bench, reminds him of the name of the innkeeper's wife. He says her name and the name of her father, To this day, says Father, I cannot forget the name, I don't know why. Where do you bury the innkeeper's wife, we ask, though we know he's not going to reveal to us where she lies, though we in fact already discover the story years ago in a book in his library, we ask him again and again where they bury the innkeeper's dead wife. After we discover the story in a book in Father's library, we're uncertain for a long time whether Father is indeed making it up each time he, who in the book is named Moishe, tells us of his journey here to the farm close to Jedenew, of the snowstorm, the coachman, who is supposedly Krystowczyk, who in the book is named Mikita, of the white horse, or whether the story in the book doesn't just tell Father's story after people perhaps pass it on for years and years beyond the borders of our houses and farms close to Jedenew and perhaps even also beyond the borders of Jedenew and ultimately write it down and print it, so that it becomes a genuine story. For a long time we are not in agreement about it and talk and quarrel for a few months until we ultimately decide that Father, who is much younger than the book, as we realize only late, only after months, steals the story, but we're also not absolutely certain, even though the book is evidently already so old that even our grandparents are still children when it appears, and so, after all the years that Father tells us his story again and again at many opportunities, early in the morning when he visits us in our rooms waking up much too early and restless, still half-asleep, tired, or excitedly wide-awake, so as to tell us the story until we fall back asleep, late in the evening by the fireplace or outside by the pond, we want to learn finally at least where the three, the coachman, or rather: Krystowczyk, Father and Wasznar, who is still young back then, bury the innkeeper's wife. Each time Father tells the story, supposedly his story, Anna says: This woman isn't anywhere, don't believe him, and contrary to our agreement, for we agree never to let anything show, and neither to betray to Father nor to make him suspect that we know the story isn't his story, can't be his story, she says: She doesn't exist, the innkeeper's dead wife doesn't exist. He's just making it all up, she says quickly, so as to turn away and back to Father at once to continue listening to him nonetheless with just as much interest as we others, waiting for him to stop protesting against Anna's joyful accusations. Impatiently waiting to see whether he doesn't reveal it this time after all, even though she knows, perhaps even knows much better than we others, who always try to maintain a little more illusion than Anna does, that he, even if he now perhaps indeed names such a place where the three bury the innkeeper's dead wife, can only make up this place. That this place does not exist. Where does the woman lie, we ask him as always. He never answers.

She gasps out: And so I leave the treehouse, as you do, earlier and earlier from night to night, and go the way from the treehouse to the clearing as you do more and more quickly from night to night, and go a less and less haphazard way to the clearing each night, and though I must sometimes search awhile until I find the clearing, I always find the clearing, always find the clearing a relatively short time after I leave the treehouse, and always find the clearing, as you do too, in a shorter time than on the night before, and ultimately come to the clearing tonight without any detour within only a few moments, and tonight find, only a few moments after I leave the treehouse, Zygmunt. She says: He's lying in the middle of the clearing on his back. She says: No doubt it's the Jedenew farmers who put him there, standing at the edge of the clearing I think: For whatever reason. She says: Scarcely do I see Zygmunt lying there when it's clear to me that I must not come out of the grain field into the clearing. Must not go to him. I must not even remain there at all, and must run away at once, run back to the treehouse as quickly and as quietly as possible, she says: It's clear to me that I must not move closer to Zygmunt, must not leave the grain field, and so I step, scarcely do I see him lying there, out of the grain field into the clearing, go to Zygmunt without looking around, looking only at Zygmunt the whole time, without looking to the right or to the left, and come closer and touch Zygmunt carefully on his foot to check if he's awake and come closer and look carefully into Zygmunt's face to check if he's awake, and grasp sleeping, lifeless Zygmunt under his arms from behind and pull him up into my arms and carry him in my arms without thinking backward into the grain field toward the treehouse and stumble and stagger forward and backward through the grain field toward the treehouse, fall with Zygmunt in my arms again and again to the left and to the right in the grain field and ultimately lose hold of Zygmunt as I elude Krystowczyk's grasp from the grain field at the last moment, dodging to the right or to the left in the grain field. In the treehouse, with her back leaning against the treehouse walls, Anna collapses and takes a deep breath, she says: I lose hold of Zygmunt, perhaps it's Krystowczyk who knocks him out of my arms, without Zygmunt I start to run without thinking. I think: Back to the treehouse, back here as directly and as quickly as possible, and think of Zygmunt again for the first time only when I'm already sitting back here in the treehouse, leaning against the wall, I think: I lose him, and now think: To want to bring him here with me is perfectly mad. I think: To leave him lying there when I lose him is the only reasonable thing to do, to want to bring him here to the treehouse with me is completely mad, she says: They follow me, she says: They run after me through the field toward here as directly, as quickly as possible. She falls asleep. She talks in her sleep, she says: The only reasonable thing to do, she says: Very well. Once. Whispers to herself: Very well, twice, again and again, then she lapses into silence, falls asleep. And while Anna is falling asleep, the barking and whimpering, the yowling of the soldiers' dogs, the voices of the Jedenew farmers penetrate to the treehouse from the field. On this evening, on the last evening in the garden behind the house, Zygmunt swims in the pond behind the house and laughs and screams and squeals with pleasure when we throw him in, as always, and naturally old Wasznar is there. Leaning against the back of the house he sits on the bench, he is silent and old and so tired that, after sitting awhile against the back of the house, he falls asleep again and again without us noticing. Naturally Father is there, he tells us: The Kradejew veterinarian clears his throat and in the silence takes a second sip from his glass of water, while Sapetow looks at him and asks him softly to begin to speak, to begin to report. The Kradejew veterinarian takes his time, nervously holds a sip of water for a long time in his mouth before he swallows, he looks at us nervously one after another, and Father stands up, goes to the window, says to us in winter: How quickly the pond freezes over this year, or says to us in summer: Don't you want to go swimming soon, tomorrow, the day after tomorrow, or says to us on the last evening: And then the Kradejew veterinarian no longer has to be asked twice. He swallows, takes a deep breath, he says, he lies, says Father: Not one of the animals, says the Kradejew veterinarian, that you supposedly slaughter out of necessity on the farms of Sapetow, Kaczmarek, Krystowczyk, Varta, Sieminski, Geniek, Dzielski and Sobuta is seriously ill. Neither seriously nor in any way ill, every single one of these animals, over two hundred and fifty head of livestock, is in perfect health, and every single one of these over two-hundred-and-fifty head of livestock is among the best of the farm, all in perfect health, says, lies the Kradejew veterinarian, says Father. He says: He takes a sip of water, adjusts his glasses, stands up briefly, motions to Sapetow with a wave of his hand to remain seated when Sapetow wants to stand up to let the Kradejew veterinarian pass, because he believes the Kradejew veterinarian wants to stand up, wants to be let past, but he gestures to Sapetow that he wants to sit down again in a moment, and so the Kradejew veterinarian only smoothes his pants, sits back down, takes out his pocket watch, says nervously: All in perfect health, checks the time with a brief glance from half-closed eyes, clears his throat, puts away the pocket watch, clears his throat, rests his elbows on the table or rests his palms on the seat of the chair or rests his underarms, folded on the counter in front of his upper body, on the counter, leans back and clears his throat, says: The gentlemen Sapetow, Kaczmarek, Krystowczyk, Varta, Sieminski, Geniek, Dzielski and Sobuta approach me already weeks ago and request that I occasionally carry out examinations on the best of their pigs, sheep, goats, and then check if you three, most of the time only a few days later, supposedly slaughter out of necessity in fact precisely those pigs that I, most of the time only a few days earlier, register as being in perfect health and moreover as the best among all the pigs that the gentlemen own. The gentlemen here request that I check what is actually happening there on their farms when you three, who by now, indeed for years already, know nearly all the pigs, sheep, goats of all those farms close to Jedenew almost better than the respective owners do, come to examine the animals at the behest of the Nadice garrison, because you three supposedly determine a few months ago that here on the Jedenew farms pig plague is rampant, though it appears nowhere else, on not a single other pig farm this side of Bisa this year or last. Because you, as the gentlemen suspect for several weeks already, are seemingly blindly marking and slaughtering only the best of the animals, the gentlemen request that I check, impartially of course, whether you, when you determine here close to Jedenew in the last months the presence of a rampant, downright galloping pig plague on nearly every single Jedenew pig farm and thereby seemingly arbitrarily slaughter whole stockyards, have them removed by the soldiers of the Nadice garrison, claim that all this is only for the very best of the farms of Sapetow, Kaczmarek, Krystowczyk, Varta, Sieminski, Geniek, Dzielski and Sobuta and for the well-being of the farm-owning families. That I check whether you don't thereby act to your own advantage in the eyes of the garrison and even proceed, as it seems to the gentlemen, exclusively at the behest of and to the advantage of the garrison. And whether in what you're doing during the last weeks, you act even to some extent rightly. Incidentally, says, lies the Kradejew veterinarian, incidentally now suddenly serene, says Father, the Kradejew veterinarian lifts his coffee cup, sets his coffee cup back on the saucer, clears his throat, says, lies, says Father: It probably interests you that rumors are circulating according to which the Nadice garrison is being dissolved within the next seven days, as well as all other garrisons this side of Bisa within the next seven days. I think that interests you perhaps and, says the Kradejew veterinarian, now fully relaxed, says Father, we all think it should also interest you that these days in Nadice, in regard to the question of who is taking the place of the Russian garrisons in Ladow and Nadice and Boiberice and Kradejew and Julowice and anywhere at all this side of Bisa, in Jedenew too, there remains scarcely any doubt. Says, lies: And that there is also no question in such a case how your chances stand of getting away, I think, don't you think so too, and so when we jump up, run away, our punch glasses fall into the water or shatter on the wooden dock or spill out over Father's books. Some of the books fall into the water as we run away, we do not breathe. The place is close to Jedenew, in the evening we count the mosquito bites on our legs and braid each other's hair, get to take turns holding crushed ice in a towel on Marek's eyebrow. At night we crouch, crammed into the pantry.

Only moments after Anna returns from the fields to the treehouse for the last time, we hear from the darkness below the treehouse the voices of the Jedenew farmers and the panting of the soldiers' dogs coming toward us in the treehouse, scarcely does Anna, murmuring, half-asleep in sadness, finish recounting what happens in the fields when the Jedenew farmers stand below the treehouse, gasping for air. Scarcely does Anna say: They follow me, say: They run after me through the field toward here without losing time, naturally without wanting to catch me before I reach the treehouse, they only want to find us, nothing else, and while Anna, whispering Zygmunt's name again and again to herself, is falling asleep, we hear the Jedenew farmers gradually coming to rest below the treehouse, the dogs sniffing the ground in the woods around our tree, the tree trunk, our tracks in the leaves and everywhere in the moss of the surrounding area. The Jedenew farmers and some soldiers they bring along, standing in the leaves below the treehouse, take pains to whisper, even though they know well enough that in the silence of the woods we can hear them already from a distance up in the treehouse, every single whisper, every moment, and then they surround us and look silently up toward us for a few minutes, and remain standing, looking upward, with their hands on their foreheads screening their eyes so as to be able to see up to the treehouse against the sun rising behind us for the last time, we hear, they laugh, clap one another on the shoulder and, laughing, shout several times: A treehouse, and turning to the soldiers waiting silently behind them, laughing a bit more softly, several times in German: A treehouse. One of them finds the block of wood left over from building the treehouse on the ground in the woods under the ferns, weighs it in his hand and then, amid the applause of the others, throws the block of wood without the necessary thrush's whistle up to us in the treehouse, and the block of wood remains lying between us. Some of the others shoot, once, twice, perhaps three times, with shotguns or rifles into the air and twice from below into the treehouse floor, perhaps only for fun, they roar with laughter, and Anna, wild Anna, big Anna, brave Anna, strong Anna, eternally disappointed and hysterical, screaming and yelling Anna, Pirate Anna moves in her sleep, twitches her eyelids in pain in her sleep as in a dream, alone in

KEVIN VENNEMANN

the end, and she moves her hand by reflex in a dream to her chest. And an ice-cold wind blows through the treetops, autumn is coming soon. Winter is coming soon, it's growing calm, and an ice-cold wind blows over the fields still lying fallow or already harvested or long since ripe for harvest, from the treehouse on clear days like this one it's possible to see across the blue, billowing and fully tilled fields to the other side of the ridge, to the far end. On this side of the dirt road stand cabbage and turnips in long rows in the fields, carrots, potatoes, and beginning on the ridge, which encloses the fields and our house and Wasznar and Antonina's farm in a basin, lie the woods. Here at the edge of the woods, directly behind the garden behind our house, directly below the treehouse it is as lonely and silent as always. The woods are as lonely and silent and black and impenetrably black as always, the valley lies scarcely ten meters below the ridge and is, strictly speaking, naturally not a valley, but we call the valley the valley since always, as far back as I can remember. And beyond what is still the valley even today, even now for one more moment, one more moment, at the far end, begin Sapetow's fields, then those of Krystowczyk, two former partisans, says Marek six nights and five days ago to Anna and Zygmunt and me, but by now and since then nothing more than conforming, secret patriots, Marek says now, here, from the clearing in the field Marek points to the place on the ridge where the dirt road leads onto the ridge and runs into the street to Jedenew, or now, here, from the wooden dock Marek points to the street that brings him to Jedenew the next day to pick up Julia from the practice

of the Jedenew doctor, or on the wooden dock points to
Zygmunt, cries: Now it's your turn, and together with
Father, laughing, throws him by his arms and legs into
the pond for fun, Zygmunt squeals with pleasure, Marek
says: And today they are glad just to be left in peace if
they only have to do a little dirty work for it. At the edge
of the woods it is as lonely and silent as always. The fog
descends, the woods are as lonely and silent and black
and impenetrably black as always, Anna, her hand on
her chest, seems to be asleep, everything else around
me blurs in the fog: the muffled laughter below the
treehouse and the barking of the dogs, the excited
thrusting of the dogs' snouts in the piles of leaves full of
our scents and food scraps all around our tree with the
treehouse in it, what remains, just outside of the woods,
scarcely a hundred meters away, of Wasznar and
Antonina's farm, Antonina's shining white dress in the
pond in the garden behind our house, Julia's nightshirt
just beside it, the still glowing fire-heap in the garden
behind our house, those one or two soldiers who have to
do sentry duty behind our house or outside the door that
leads out of the kitchen into the garden, the fields,
Father's car on the dirt road, a shiver accompanies the
moment of transition. Anna, her hand on her chest, is
fast asleep. I don't want to wake her and so I crouch on
the treehouse floor, Anna's upper body in my arms, and
so I stand up and, shivering, carefully let Anna's upper
body sink onto the frost-white treehouse floor. I see from
the only half-finished treehouse our fields in the fog,
deeply snow-covered and lying fallow, us in them, four
of us playing, see the fields green, billowing and bearing

grain growing in the fog, our fields and five of us in them, the fields shining golden and ripe and light brown against the dark autumn sun and six of us in them and in the fog, see the fields hidden under a blanket of snow. See us lying in the fields and walking along the dirt road and see four of us playing hide-and-seek in the fields for many years, five of us for four years, six of us for a short summer, and see us in the deeply snow-covered fields waging eternal snowball fights, a swarm of wasps in the snow, says Wasznar or says Father or Marek to us, Krystowczyk perhaps. I stand in the hole in the treehouse that is one day supposed to be the door of the treehouse, and I think of Marek, when he says that on that morning a few days ago, the last morning, neither he nor Krystowczyk nor, at that moment, anyone else could precisely know what's going to happen in Jedenew and close to Jedenew and anywhere else at all. And so I am the only one who finds out, for the last time everything once more. I look across the fields and to our house, to the smoldering something that, after six nights and five days, still remains of Wasznar and Antonina's farm close to Jedenew in the fog, the fireplace in Wasznar and Antonina's living room, the fireplace in the kitchen, the banister that leads down into the cellar, one or two wall elements in the back, the partitions and a charred door-frame that leads out of the front of the house into the front garden, into the yard, past the former barn and through the dense poplars to our home, and through the snow and across a scarcely ankle-high, dark-green meadow full of daisies, past the bench on which Kacia sits, knits or scrubs pots, into our kitchen, the windows shatter, and nothing is as before. And so I take Pirate Anna's pirate-hand in my hand and squeeze it tightly, let it go and lower the rope-ladder through the opening for the treehouse door from the eternally unfinished treehouse. One of the soldiers' dogs begins to yowl when it hears the rope-ladder falling, and some of the Jedenew farmers see me, laugh loudly, then all is silent and there is nothing more to hear, nothing more to see, and so I stand in the eternally roofless treehouse, in the treehouse opening that no longer gets a door, and hear and say nothing, there is nothing to say. I do not breathe.

THE ART OF THE NOVELLA